FAREWELL TO DEJLA

Farewell to Dejla

STORIES OF IRAQI JEWS AT
HOME AND IN EXILE

Tova Murad Sadka

Dedicated to the memory of my mother, Fawziya,
whose wisdom and goodness are my life guidance.

Cover and interior design: Sarah Olson
Cover photograph: Glasshouse Images/BJ Formento

Chicago Review Press Incorporated
814 North Franklin Street
Chicago, Illinois 60610
ISBN 978-0-89733-581-2

© 2009 Tova Murad Sadka

Printed in the U.S.A.

Library of Congress Cataloging-in-Publication Data on
file with the publisher.

Contents

I: Jews In Iraq

The Status Quo

The rabbi sipped at his sherbet. Apricot-flavored sherbet, rose-wa-tered, ice-topped, floating in golden-edged glass. Some recipe against Baghdad's dry heat. He leaned back on the sofa and watched the ceiling fan set at its highest. It could have been bearably warm were it not for his long thick robe, the underwear trousers and the huge turban. Lucky European rabbis dress like ordinary men.

A hesitant tap at the door.

"Come in," the rabbi sighed.

Daoud with his bewildered look and tied tongue.

"Now, what is it, Daoud?"

"The policeman returned the rice."

"What?"

"You told me to send twenty kilos of rice to the new captain of the Shorea. He sent it back."

"He sent it back, hm." The rabbi bobbed his head. "We had no problem with Ahmad."

"What?" Daoud looked perplexed.

"Ahmad, the previous police captain."

"Ah."

"Twenty kilos of rice for the first three months," the rabbi murmured and sipped at his sherbet, "twenty of sugar, the next three
months, then the twenty of flour, then the two trunks of dates."

"This one is better, rabbi, honest, no bribes."

The rabbi laughed, choking on his sherbet and splattering the
drink on his robe. To enjoy his laugh or attend to his robe? He chose
the latter as Daoud frantically grabbed a towel and wiped the drops.

"Daoud," the rabbi began patiently. "The captain's salary is not
enough to buy shoes for his ten children, maybe fifteen or twenty,
who knows. And he would spare the 'wealthy Jews' as the Moslems
call us?"

"No, rabbi."

The rabbi became thoughtful. "Now listen, Daoud. In ten days,
we will have the king's birthday, so send the captain twenty kilos of
sugar for the occasion."

"Twenty kilos of sugar."

"Yes. Maybe he likes sugar better." The rabbi chuckled.

"You think so, rabbi?"

"Go Daoud, go now, it is my nap hour." The rabbi shook his
head.

Were gullible employees really better? No ambitious mischief behind one's back, no treacherous schemes . . . except for the ones due
to unwitting stupidity? The unconscious, yet efficiently troublesome
improvisions of the gullible.

Daoud shuffled off and closed the door behind him. The rabbi
took off his turban and stationed it on the end table. Then he pulled
off his shoes and lay down on the sofa. No other furniture in the room
except for a desk and a chair. The rabbi's glance fell on the morning
newspaper. Some skirmish between Jews and Arabs in Palestine. The
British occupation forces. . . . Did the Shorea captain sense a loop in
the local status quo?

The rabbi closed his eyes and started his silent sleep mantra—his
birthday, day and month repeated over and over again. But his mind
drifted, roamed everywhere and nowhere, chasing off his sleep. He
thought of his bare office. And when bare is the place, bare is the

soul! Some furniture should be bought to make the place look decent. The Majlis—the Jewish council—should allow the expense. Again he began his sleep mantra. He needed his strength. He would concentrate fully and sleep would finally soothe his mind and body. It didn't. An unpleasant thought buzzing and buzzing like a fly. The returned twenty kilos of rice.

Protection bribes for police captains were as old as the world, that is the Jewish world, its means for safety and survival. The rabbi took care of the two captains presiding over the Jewish quarters of the old city. The same exact bribe for both, on a regular basis—a good recipe to avoid problems. But this new one in the Shorea. . . . "Let's not worry, let's wait and see," the rabbi told himself, "let's not think about it."

He did not think about it and benevolent sleep enveloped him.

An urgent knock at the door and Daoud came in, blurting, "The captain returned the twenty kilos of sugar."

"Hm." The rabbi sipped at his sherbet. It tasted warm and somewhat sour. "Hm," he repeated and remained silent for a few seconds. "Get me some more ice," he finally said and extended his glass to Daoud.

Daoud slowly picked up the glass, looked at the rabbi and rushed out.

He came right back, tickling the ice cubes in the golden-edged glass. "Here, rabbi."

The rabbi extended his hand. "Time to see Jawad," he murmured to himself. "Daoud, call Jawad's office and make an appointment for me. The sooner the better."

"Jawad, rabbi?"

"Yes, Jawad Muntassar. Baghdad Chief of Police."

"Yes, rabbi."

"Wait, just a second, Daoud." The rabbi picked up the morning newspaper and read a little. The skirmishes between Jews and Arabs in Palestine did not look that serious. "Don't call Jawad's office yet," he finally said.

It would be better to wait and see. Groping in the dark and taking measures, versus studying the situation and then preempting the opponent's strategy before it took shape; he opted for the latter.

"Don't call Jawad's office yet," he repeated. "Let's wait and see."

The door burst open, and a large man barged in with breathless Daoud after him.

"I told him you are busy, rabbi, but he . . . ," Daoud began.

"Rabbi, please." The man's voice shook. He was a butcher. The white, slightly bloodied apron, the muscled arms . . .

"It's all right, Daoud," the rabbi said. He turned to the butcher. "What is it, my friend?"

"Rabbi, I am afraid." The butcher breathed hard. "Today, a police captain came to inspect my shop. It never happened before."

The rabbi nodded.

"The captain said I don't keep good hygiene. I showed him how everything was clean, immaculate clean, but he just shook his head. Finally he said he wants to see me in his office this Friday, to discuss the matter. You know I keep everything clean, rabbi, you know that."

Again the rabbi bobbed his head. "Did the captain come alone?" he asked.

"Yes."

"Did he go to the other butchers' shops?"

"Yes."

"Did he ask the other butchers to come to his office?"

"No."

"He will," the rabbi murmured to himself. Then he turned to the butcher. "I . . . I will try to take care of it. Don't go to his office on Friday unless I tell you. Return to your shop and wait for my word."

"Rabbi . . . ," the butcher pleaded.

"I will take care of it. I will try."

"Thank you rabbi, thank you."

"Now Daoud," the rabbi said as soon as the butcher left. "Call Jawad's office and make the appointment for today. Today."

"Yes, rabbi. Let me get your sherbet."

"No Daoud, not now."

He would enjoy it better after seeing Jawad. As Baghdad's Chief of Police, Jawad knew that his captains were bribed for the Jews' protection. Hopefully he would take care of the matter.

The rabbi walked the paved narrow street, with Daoud on his right and another employee on his left. There was no need for a taxi as Jawad's office was three streets away. The two-story houses provided enough shade, but the thick robe, the underwear trousers and the huge turban. . . . Lucky European rabbis who dress like ordinary men.

The majestic two-story police headquarters had two huge columns in front. One policeman stood by each column. The rabbi slowed his steps and nodded to Daoud who went over to one of the policemen.

"The rabbi is here," Daoud announced.

The policeman left his post and went inside. Immediately Jawad appeared at the threshold, tall, slim, jovial and mustached. "Welcome, welcome, rabbi. Such an honor." He bent his tall figure and extended his hand.

The rabbi shook the extended hand and bowed his head. Jawad's good graces were secured by the Majlis. The rabbi did not feed the big fish. They were the responsibility of the Majlis.

"Come into my office, please. Such an honor, rabbi."

The Moslems' smooth tongue. The sharp dagger at short notice or no notice at all. The rabbi went into Jawad's office while Daoud and the other employee remained in the hallway.

Jawad helped the rabbi into an armchair. Did he look like he needed Jawad's help, the rabbi wondered? He was only fifty years old. It's the thick robe and the huge turban. The European rabbis. . . .

Jawad's office was large and well-furnished. A sofa, four chairs, a desk and a cupboard. And it was so cool. Not only the ceiling fan, but a desk fan took care of the hot air. A good idea. Two fans working at one time. The rabbi should have the same in his office. The Majlis should allow the expense.

"Some sherbet, rabbi?" Jawad was all smiles as he caressed his mustache.

"No thank you, chief. I would not take much of your time. I just came to thank you for the new police captain of the Shorea."

Jawad remained silent, and the rabbi continued.

"He is very good. He is honest. We send him twenty kilos of sugar on occasion of the king's birthday and he refused to take them."

Jawad's pleasant features remained impassive. There was a moment of silence before the rabbi continued.

"He is also very concerned about the hygiene in the butchers' shops. He went to inspect them himself."

Jawad looked perplexed.

"One by one." The rabbi stressed his words.

"Hm." Jawad looked thoughtful. Then he shook his head. "I am so sorry to disappoint you, rabbi. This captain was sent to the Shorea on a temporary basis and we have to transfer him. The poor Moslem district of Ashouria lacks all hygiene, much more than your district. It needs someone like him, honest and conscious. So we need to transfer him, soon, this week maybe. I am sorry, rabbi."

"I understand. The welfare of the more needy comes first."

"Now, rabbi, some sherbet maybe?"

"Yes, thank you. It is hot."

As soon as he finished his sherbet, the rabbi took leave of Jawad and headed toward his office. Noon already. Time for a good long nap. Should Jawad receive something extra for his congenial welcome to the rabbi? He could get the twenty kilos of rice that anyway would have gone to the Shorea captain. But it might create a precedent. And the Majlis might object. Better to leave the decision to the Majlis; Jawad was its responsibility. What mattered was that the status quo was still in place.

For now!

Shoula and the Moslem Man

Nazim was passing by her room when suddenly he stopped at the threshold. "Why do you keep your curtain open, Shoula?" he asked. "You are in full view of the neighbors."

She smiled, noting the concern on his face. "Because," she spoke slowly, "because, brother dear, I like to have some light in my room."

"At least, close the curtain half-way."

She grinned. "How about quarter-way, dear brother?"

"All you know is how to tease," he complained, shook his head and walked off.

"No one has a view of my room except the grandmother across the street," she called after him.

No response. Did he hear, or didn't he? Oh yes, he did hear.

She shrugged, walked to the curtain and closed it a quarter. A little more than a quarter; she was feeling magnanimous. Let him check on his wife. He had no business bothering her.

True, there was much proximity between the neighbors and consequently little privacy; Shoula knew that. But it was the structure of old Baghdad; the winding streets were less than four yards wide and all the houses were attached. Also, the houses' second floors protruded, providing shade for the pedestrians, and most had at least one room with a window facing the street. Shoula happened to occupy the only one in her house. Across the street, right opposite hers, was the one belonging to the neighbors' grandmother who hardly used it; she must be busy with the children and grandchildren. As to pedestrians in the street: they could hardly see Shoula except if she stood or sat very close to the window.

It was a Jewish neighborhood and she liked to sit knitting by the window.

Sometimes her mother would join her and they would chat while enjoying the street scene. There were the young boys and girls going to school, the men hurrying to their businesses. It was a small neighborhood and Shoula knew quite a few of the frequent passersby. The family across the street were a young couple with three children, the husband's mother and his two bachelor brothers. The bachelors would hurry, early to work, and early back home. They seemed conceited, walking erect, their heads high and wet with hair cream, their shirts halfway open, showing off their hairy chests. And they were young, in their late twenties at most, while Shoula was thirty-five, going on thirty-six. But she was still very attractive.

She went to study her reflection in the cupboard's mirror. She was pretty if not very pretty. Her small black eyes were lively and her beautiful brown hair long and thick. And she was slim, rather small-breasted, but tall and well-shaped.

She left her room and headed downstairs. Her mother was preparing dinner and Shoula offered to make the salad.

"Do you know . . . ?" Shoula began.

"I know. Nazim told me about it."

That was not what Shoula had in mind. But just as well.

"I explained to him," her mother went on, "that you don't open the curtain when you dress, and that the window across the street is the grandmother's. And your bed is in the corner, completely out of sight."

Shoula's mother sided with her most of the time; she felt sorry for her, because by now Shoula was officially declared a spinster. What Baghdadian Jewish bachelor would marry a thirty-five-year-old?

"Of course, if you don't mind, Shoula, you could leave the curtain half-way open. And you could close it when you're not in the room."

There was diplomatic Mother, siding with Shoula yet . . . always a yet. Conciliatory? All right; that was what mothers were supposed to be. An open curtain indeed! Her mother and brother should worry about something far more serious, that is if she were to tell them about it. It had happened twice and it disturbed her a great deal. Once as she absentmindedly came to sit by the window, she saw a man urinating in the street corner. He was dressed in a suit, his head wrapped with the Moslem kaffiya. He lifted up his head and, seeing her, he began manipulating himself, pressing his prick against the wall. She immediately backed inside her room, scared and disgusted. From then on she became careful, watching the street before sitting at the window. It was not often that Moslems passed by the Jewish quarter and she hoped it was a one-time thing. But it happened again when, after inspecting the street and seeing that the coast was clear, she sat knitting by the window. But as soon as she raised her eyes from her knitting, she saw the same Moslem watching her and again pressing his prick against the wall. She had hurried inside the room, sunk onto her bed and tried to steady her heartbeat. And she had decided to stop sitting by the window for at least a month before trying it again. He would certainly stop. Meanwhile he was depriving her of her window and she visualized taking a hammer and cracking his head.

"Don't put in too much vinegar." Her mother's words brought her mind back to the salad.

"All right."

The sudden shrill cries of Nazim's children. Teffeh was four, a pretty girl, and Nouri, a well-developed boy, was two. Shoula considered them spoiled, but Mother disagreed. Dola, their mother, would soon bring them to the table for dinner, to mess up and disturb. "They are like your own children," Mother once said.

"No, they are not like my own children," Shoula had snapped. "They are Nazim and Dola's. They are not my children."

"I just meant they are living here with us," Mother's voice had faltered, but Shoula would not ease the situation; she just headed to her room and left Mother to reach her own conclusions, whatever they were.

"Could you put the bread on the table?" Shoula's mother asked.

"Sure," Shoula said and did.

The table was set in the backyard porch. It was early May, but already hot. The smell of the pinkish bean flowers caught Shoula's nostrils. She sniffed the air and sighed. Amazing how the fragrance of flowers sent her mind wandering into a strange, beautiful land: tall sturdy trees and a cloudy sunrise giving a pinkish glow to the leaves, while a silvery river flowed in the background.

"Nazim," Mother's sharp call brought Shoula back to the backyard porch. "Dinner is ready."

Nazim and Dola came, Nouri in Dola's arms, Teffeh on Nazim's shoulder.

Dola had her brown hair up, her long neck showing. She was rather pretty and soft-spoken. She and Dola were not friends, so to speak. You could not have a conversation with Dola except about her children; as to other matters, she was Nazim's mouthpiece. "Fine," Mother would say. "As a daughter-in-law, Dola is not bad at all. And she is a good decent wife to Nazim, which is important." Nazim was good-looking, tall and slim, with large greenish eyes and bushy black hair. He had a wide nose and his nostrils would dilate and quiver whenever he got excited or angry.

Nazim was silent. Exhibiting his displeasure with her? She should check his nostrils, she laughed to herself. And Dola was mute. In solidarity? There was some dutiful wife.

The dinner passed in silence, except for some banal comments by or about the children. Mother contributed the most. Shoula could feel the tense atmosphere, and she returned silence with silence, distance by distance. However, she was set on enjoying her favorite meal, okra with meat and rice, and she ate and ate, more than usual. Then she and mute Dola helped Mother clear the table. That done, Shoula left the back porch. She did not, as usual, join Nazim as he listened to the news on the radio in the hall. What was there to hear? Some new head of state in Germany called Hitler and he hated the Jews. So what else was new? She went straight to her room. She did not like sewing or knitting at night. She would just read a little, then go to sleep. She picked up the American romance and ventured into that world where. . . .

She woke up to the sound of noises from the street. It was Wednesday and Dola would take the children and spend the day with her family. It would be nice and quiet for a change. But Shoula actually liked the children. It could be she loved them—that is when they were not grouchy.

She stood up and opened the window curtain. Young boys and girls were hurrying to school. Was it that long ago that she herself was a teenage student? The way time flies. She remembered the first matches suggested for her when her paternal Uncle Shalom decided they were not good enough: this one came from a low-class family, the other had a retarded relative, then. . . . Her father had passed away when she was fourteen years old. He had owned a small but thriving printing business and when he suddenly died of a heart attack, Uncle Shalom took it upon himself to supervise the family affairs. He helped Nazim take charge of the printing business and advised Shoula's mother on all financial matters. He was wealthy, living in a huge house with a sleep-in maid. Yet her mother claimed he found faults with the suitors for fear he would be asked to help with the dowry. He specially objected when the suitors were not well off. But most of the well-off ones were old, and her mother did not want her to end up a young widow. At that time she was flattered that her uncle and mother would not sell her short. But time passed and she became anxious that she might not marry or raise a family of her own. When Uncle Shalom suddenly died and the heirs took over, she forgot all about help with her dowry. She had her small one, provided by her mother, and it was amazing how the quality of suitors declined by the day. What annoyed her was that Nazim went on and married, when he was only three years her senior. Jewish men did not marry before their sisters, though the sisters might be much younger. Sometimes, the brothers even provided the dowries, that is when the father was dead, or had no money. It was rare that daughters did not marry, but when it happened the standing-on-line brothers often remained single as well. It was not right to bring a bride into the house, when the living-in-daughter had not married yet; it would be like bringing a rival for her and making her feel like a second-class citizen. But Nazim would not wait; he went straight out and married a distant family relative. And he took over his father's business. Of course her mother saw to it that he gave Shoula some of the income. Two years before, Shoula herself wanted to work at the printing office, suggesting that Nazim could dispense with his assistant. She had plenty of time on her hands. She helped her mother, did some knitting and sewing, and visited family or friends. Sometimes Nazim and Dola would go to a movie and they would ask her to join them. She cut down on visiting her girl cousins, after that episode with Cousin Alice. She had gone to congratulate Alice on the birth of her son when she heard Alice tell her sister to cover the baby's face. She understood that Alice feared her evil eye because she, Shoula, was unmarried and had no children. She had cried enough that day, and though she tried to hide the tears, her mother noted her red eyes and insisted on knowing the reason.

"I see," her mother said. "Listen to me, dear daughter. These stupid women are afraid of everyone's eye, not only yours. Besides, you can hit a baby with the evil eye not necessarily by looking at him. And like I told you many times, you will be provided for if something happens to me. The house is in my name and I inherited the business as my ktuba [the money pledged to the wife on marriage, to be given to her in case of the husband's death.] And when I die you will inherit half. I know it's not much, but at least you're modestly provided for. Some families don't do even that. They leave the sisters at the brothers' mercy."

"So my father was wise to put the house in your name."

"Most Jewish men do that. As to the small business, it hardly covered my ktuba."

Nazim vehemently objected to Shoula working in the printing business. "Do you see any working girl in our class? And from the lower classes, nothing but seamstresses or the like."

"There is always a first," Shoula kept saying, but no one wanted to listen. Not even her mother. "It's in the old market, dear," her mother said. "Only men are there and most of them are Moslems. If it was working from the house, then it would be all right."

Of course Nazim told her wishes to the aunts, the cousins and others. And they mocked her. Even worse, they must have felt sorry for her. She thought she heard her aunt whispering, "Poor girl. She should have married." Let them all go to hell. So now she was the ordained spinster. No man would want to marry a thirty-six-year-old. She might not bring children. Oh yes somebody would. A certain widower in his sixties had come by recently, with two teenaged girls and a nine-year-old boy. His nose reaching his belly, his mouth from one ear to the other! She visualized marrying him and he would sleep snoring through his enormous open mouth. And then she would bring a rag to stuff in his mouth.

She should not have mean thoughts. It was not the man's fault that his belly was so set upward and his mouth joining his ears. She did not really care about marriage. Some lousy good-for-nothing thinking he is the master of the world and imposing his will on her. But she longed, she longed for the warmth and the intimacy of a partner, and she often daydreamed, knowing well that none of her dreams would come true. Did she ever love someone, did she ever vie for someone? There was Elisha, who married a rich girl. There was Neemat, who would not venture before his sisters and as soon as the third one married, he became engaged. Of course there were some handsome and wealthy married men whose wives might suddenly die and. . . . Oh God forgive her, God forbid that she would live off someone else's misery. She was not pretty pretty, and her dowry was so small. Why should women need dowries? The man is given a wife and money as well! With the Moslems it is the husband who gives the dowry. Reading those American magazines, she got a glimpse of that faraway world, with none of the restrictions on women, none of the taboos on their work or education. She would daydream about a handsome man who was clever, wise and loving. And there would be encounters where she loved him, clashed or argued with him but all the episodes would end with him lovingly capitulating.

She jerked herself away from the window and went inside, her heart palpitating. The Moslem man! So now she would not be able to ever sit by the window. Even that was too much for her? Anger squeezed her chest as she visualized cracking the man's head with a hammer. She sat on her bed and steadied her heartbeat. A minute before, she had absently sunk into the chair by the window and there he was, looking toward her, his hand inside his pants, his eyes so intense. For quite a while it hadn't happened, and she had almost forgotten about him. That was why she had not inspected the street before sitting down. From now on she would watch from behind the slightly transparent curtain. Could it be he was looking at somebody else too? There was a window on the adjoining street which also faced the corner.

She sighed and moved backward toward the room door, crawled forward to station herself behind the curtain. The man was still there, but he was facing the wall, his jerking body bent sideways. She would not tell her mother nor Nazim. What for? She was glad her mother had not come to sit by the window lately, and she would be extra careful from now on. She would sneak behind the curtain, see if the coast was clear and then sit. Also, she might come to know his timing; he must have a schedule. He must go to work somewhere.

She came home and headed toward the kitchen, when her mother's bewildered face accosted her. "Shoula."

"Yes. Now what's the matter?"

"An hour ago I went into your room to take your knitting and looked out the window. I saw a Moslem man by the corner wall. He was urinating and then you know. . . . And he was looking toward your window."

Shoula remained silent.

"Have you ever seen him before? Terrible. . . . I mean some men urinate in the street, but this. . . . Have you ever seen him, Shoula?"

"Only once," Shoula said. She could not lie more than that.

"Could he have dared do that in his own Moslem neighborhood? Urinating, perhaps, but not the other thing. Don't sit by the window anymore, Shoula."

"Is that too much too, sitting by the window?"

"What can you do? Those Moslem men can be very nasty, and dangerous."

"All right, Mother, I won't, don't worry."

A jerk, a miserable low life, would dictate to her where to sit in her own house! A scum of the earth was depriving her of her window. Did she wish to crack his skull and split it in two halves? Would he ever disappear so she could resume her old life?

"Don't tell Nazim, Mother."

"I don't know. Maybe I should."

"He will just worry, and what for? I won't sit by the window anymore."

But her mother did tell Nazim: an hour later, he came into her room and interrogated her about the Moslem man, warning her, urging her not to sit by the window ever again.

Loud shouting and screams coming from the street. She crawled toward the window curtain and peeked. It was the Moslem man writhing and screaming. "Aw, waw, children of whores, pimps, God strike you scoundrels . . . waw waw."

She smiled.

"What are those screams? What is it, what's going on?" Nazim and her mother came to her room door.

"Don't come in, don't come in," she shouted and crawled toward them. "It's the Moslem man."

"What. . . ."

"Waw, children of whores, you just wait, scoundrels," the screams went on.

"The Moslem man who urinates in the street," she whispered. "Early this morning I spread red pepper on the wall."

"What?" Nazim cried. "Are you out of your mind? He's a Moslem. You don't know what he might do."

"He wouldn't know who did it. Maybe someone from the window on the other street. How would he know?"

"He would throw something on the house, he would. . . ." She watched Nazim's dilated nostrils and hid her smile. "Let me go to the bathroom," she said and rushed out. She hurried in, locked the door and leaned against it. She could hear Nazim's shouts. She recalled the Moslem's shrieking face, Nazim's dilated, quivering nostrils and smiled while tears gathered in her eyes.

The Rooster Crows

Ahmad woke to the crowing of the Haj's rooster—a strong, crystal-clear call vibrating into the valley. Of all the fellahin's roosters, the Haj's was the most healthy and virile. Big and thick-winged he would hop about relentlessly chasing the hens in all the fellahin's tents.

Ahmad stretched his tall body along the straw carpet. The warm drunkenness of sleep drowned his senses. He moved to Acuna's side; it was empty and the hard straw carpet scratched his white tunic. He lingered awhile, then slowly got up and went outside. Acuna was fiddling with the fire and the kettle. She was an efficient, hard-working wife.

"Shall I pour you some tea?" she asked.

"Yes."

He drank his tea, ate his bread, and snatched some yogurt from one of the boxes which Acuna would soon carry on her head as she walked toward the city. The sun, hindered by the clay fence of the Busman, had not yet reached his tent, yet the air smelled of oppressive heat. A hot wind was blowing over the plantation, but it did not smell like a sandstorm. Sandstorms were worse than winter rain and last year's was so strong that he and his sons had to hold on to the tent's posts so they would not fly off.

His two sons, Ibrahim and Ismail, and his daughter Fata, were already in the fields, turning the ground around the cucumbers, tomatoes and melons. After finishing their work there, they would head for the Kall plantation to gather the cotton crop. Acuna would take the yogurt boxes and sell them in the city. And Ahmad would remain alone in the tent. When the big loud machine started pumping and watering the valley, he would go and see if the water ran well into the furrows. Then he would come back, drink coffee and smoke hookah. Some of the fellahin might come and join him or he himself would venture into another fellah's gathering.

Acuna bent over the yogurt boxes. She bent all the way, the back heel of her bandaged feet showing from under the long black outfit. He thought of her buttocks, the wrinkles at the lower end and the folds of falling flesh above them. He wanted a new wife. Where would he get the money for the dowry? He wished he had more children to send out to work in the fields. Allah who gives and takes had blessed him with eight and left him with three. If the Jew's family came this summer, he would make extra money guarding their ranch at night. The Jew would hire no one but him; he belonged to the Jallal tribe. No one would trespass on the Jew while he was on guard; it would be like trespassing on the whole Jallal tribe. Even so, the money wouldn't be much and he wouldn't be able to save for a new wife. Everything slipped from his hand: The money for tea and coffee, for sugar, for the once-a-month meat and. . . . he couldn't afford a new wife. And who, among the bedouins his age, didn't own a second wife? Only the very poor and those two, Ali the dairy man and Mustapha the mechanic, who had stayed so long with the Jew that they ended up being like him, one-wife men. It was easy working for the Jew. Like all landlords, the Jew dealt with the fellahin on a 50 percent basis: the fellahin would sow, harvest and sell the crop, then divide the proceeds with him. But, unlike Moslem landlords, the Jew did not insist on receiving his money on time, nor did he get nasty when things went wrong. He also lived in the city and rarely stayed over at the plantation to supervise and inspect. But sometimes there were better deals around, in the amount of offered land, and Ahmad, like his fellow nomad fellahin, would seek the best proposition and carry his tent and family around, one season here, one season there.

The sun had reached the edge of the tent. There was some fire left. Ahmad went for the pot of coffee and made himself a cup. Gushes of hot air pricked his face. He held the handleless cup and sipped the strong sugarless coffee, his eyes on the far horizon. He had very strong eyesight and could see as far as Bab-el-Madina. Last week when the owner of the Kall plantation arrived, Ahmad was able to make out the car while it was still only a tiny spot of light. All the fellahin stood on the high Sadda, but none could make out the moving spot. He was physically strong as well. The other day, when Ali was struggling with a bunch of date trunks, he helped him by lifting the load in one shot and setting it on the back of the donkey. And Ali was some years his junior.

The coffee grounds stuck in Ahmad's throat. The hot air scratched his face and triggered his blood. He sat cross-legged on the bare dry land at the threshold of his tent and watched everyone pass: children, young boys and girls, men and women, all heading for the Kall plantation. Noura with the almond eyes and the pearl teeth emerged from her tent. She walked to the edge of the road and bent down to pick up her little brother, revealing the bare back heel of her bandaged feet. She lifted the child, caressed him and took him inside the tent. A smile had glowed on her moon-shaped face, a velvety chocolate-colored face, framed by the black veil. Ahmad thought of Acuna's face, its skin as hard as clay.

He sighed, stood up and looked around him. Then he went to inspect Noura's footprints on the yellow sand. He followed them closely, right and left. Then he stopped to look at the last two, near the edge of the road. Slowly he lifted his right foot and carefully planted it on the right footprint. He studied the position of the left footprint, lifted his own left foot and stamped on it. For a moment he stared at his feet right on top of Noura's footprints. The heat of the clay entered his feet and passed through his legs, up his back and into his head. He gazed at the dry endless valley. The sun hit him right on the brow. He took a deep breath, a long loud sigh from his chest. Exhausted and dazed, he dragged himself back to his tent and sat. Noura had come out of her tent, and Fata, his daughter, ran to catch up with her. Together, the two girls walked toward the Kall plantation. They were the same height, perhaps the same age. As they walked away, they were indistinguishable. Suddenly, Ahmad's heart began to race. He stood up and went inside the tent to fetch more coffee, to clear his head and help him think. But his heart raced, and he soon found himself outside, in front of Mehdi's tent.

Mehdi was tending one of his sheep. The sun had begun to roast the row of tents and the Haj's rooster was chasing the hens.

"This heat will kill our cucumbers," Mehdi said.

Ahmad could not restrain his heart's palpitations and his words ran by themselves. "We are poor, poor as beggars, with no dowries for new wives. But we have two daughters, Noura and Fata. They are the same height, maybe the same weight. They go to the Kall planta-tion together. . . ."

Mehdi looked incredulous, then bewildered, and burst into big, loud laughter. "By Allah, you are a devil, Ahmad, that is what you are. Why didn't I think of it myself? It is a gift from heaven, a blessing from Allah. But wait, Noura's dowry should go for her brother, As-sam. The boy is sixteen, maybe eighteen, maybe twenty. . . ."

"What about my Ibrahim, next year the army. He is grown up, but plenty of time for a dowry yet."

"Never heard of a daughter's dowry going to the father," Ibrahim moaned. "And do we need more mouths to feed with a new brat ev-ery year?"

"My daughter, my beautiful Fata to the old," Acuna raged to her-self.

At the edge of the calm, bright flow of Diala River, Acuna pros-trated herself on the ground, threw dust on her face and clothes and hit her chest with both fists. "Men with mercy, help me," she cried. "The daughter has drowned, vanished into the water. Diala the treacherous. Diala the diabolic had swallowed her young body, her young years. . . ."

A crowd of bedouins had gathered, and men, young and old, began to plunge into the water, disturbing the proud serenity of the silvery flow. They swam in circles, beat and splashed the water and came out breathless and dripping. "Which way did she go?" they asked Acuna.

"Here and there, my daughter, my beautiful Fata," she raved, and the men plunged again, diving and scouring the water.

Then they saw Ahmad coming. He walked quickly, followed by his son, his head high and his tall body erect. The crowd gathered around him. "Fata has drowned. Fata has drowned." His hawk eyes narrowed. He did not answer but sent a cold glance toward Acuna, walked to the shore, and with his clothes on, went into the water, and within minutes had swum to the other side of the river and climbed up the steep shore.

"Where is he going?" Acuna asked.

"To your people, Mother," Ibrahim answered. "Where else would you send her?"

The tall figure of Ahmad disappeared behind the steep shore. He walked across the vast empty land until he reached a row of tents, among them those of Acuna's people. He confronted Acuna's brother and spoke with him, man to man, in the language of men. "I want my daughter, where is she?"

"There she is." Acuna's brother pointed to one of the tents.

At the edge of the steep shore, Ahmad, followed by Fata, stopped and viewed Acuna and the crowd, their forms mingling with the high bushes. Then he plunged into the water, the girl behind him.

Early next morning, as the Haj's rooster began to crow, Ahmad set out for his long walk to the city, to buy the two new dresses for the brides, while Mehdi began his journey to the far-off Fakri Plantation to hire the tambourine for the double wedding.

The Veiled Sphinx

"**S**he is Jewish like me!" Ovadia rejoiced and immediately his imagination went loose, his heart throbbed, and that familiar chill along the back. . . . "Wait," he cried, "Don't run wild then . . . I know you." And he knew them, much too well; their visionary tricks, their wild dreams, floating him up to the sky then suddenly dropping him to the ground. No regard for broken heart or soul.

"Wait," he repeated, his eyes stuck to the undulating veiled form. "Who says she is Jewish?" If she were not, he would not venture. Heaven forbid! No Moslem girl for him; no dark vengeful fathers and brothers with long mustaches; no sharp daggers thrown from all sides. But no, she definitely is Jewish: The black cloak swaying awkwardly, the veil crumbled and twisted to the side . . . and that stumble right now! What Moslem woman wears the veil so clumsily; it's her everyday garment, as natural as her own skin and her eyes long adjusted to the dark screen. And what Moslem girl would walk the Jewish quarter? As a crossroad, maybe? Seldom or never.

She, then he, passed the large new Jewish Hospital. She, then he, slowed near the old synagogue with the shabby brick arch, the hanging lantern and the smell of rose water. Then they entered the quarter of the well-to-do:—winding streets filled with beggars and lined by two-story houses.

And why a black cloak and veil on such a lovely day? For what purpose the dark and stifling prison if not for a secret mission, some mysterious escapade? On the lookout my dear, ha? Don't tell me, I know your elders wear the cloak. But the cloak alone, without the veil. And what sort of cloak? Short and open, a mere token of modesty and conformity with the local customs, to deter the whistles and hissing of Moslem men—poor, forlorn souls, deprived of Moslem display, therefore eager for a Jewish one. While you, my dear girl . . . now, who says she is a dear girl and not a dearest elderly lady? Ah, no! Not with these narrow dainty sandals and the two protruding toes.

The girl turned right and Ovadia followed. He stroked his young beard, adjusted his trousers and shirt and stretched his five-four height to almost five-six. He entered narrow, dark unpaved streets with old shabby houses—the poor residential section where women and children sauntered with bare feet or worn-out slippers. Then the commotion of the Jewish food market. Ovadia struggled to keep the ideal three-yard distance between him and his. . . . He zigzagged amid shoppers, peddlers, loaded donkeys, vegetable boxes and chicken cages. The large bowls of pickles with their curry and cumin smell sent a sharp tickle through his nostrils. Then the sweet, soothing smell from the bakery. The market ended with the kosher chicken slaughterer where men and women stood in line, holding their fowl by the feet. A sick verdict would send the fowl back to the peddler; a healthy one would insure a quick, merciful death as only a kosher slaughterer could do it. With a new residential area in view, Ovadia was able to breathe again. He quickened his step, caught up with, then passed the veiled figure, brushing against the silky cloak. A cool tremor caught his back. He turned to find the tremor's cause and wow . . . she had crossed to the steep alley leading to the blacksmith market. Was there to be no end to her wanderings? Would she tour heaven and earth to test him? A narrow, tented street, blocking all sunlight, with tiny stores where dark muscular men worked with the red brass. A chorus of hammers pounded the utensils, hurting the ears with the music of hell. Two sharp turns and suddenly there was light. A serene, residential area with no beggars and few passersby. Ovadia lifted his chest and pushed back his oiled hair. Then he began his technique of alternately preceding, then following behind the mysterious figure, slightly brushing the veil in the process, a technique which, when duly accelerated, would ultimately blur the vision of the victim, confuse her and make her fall, fall into his arms. . . .

"Hold it, hold it!" Ovadia again rebuked his wild imagination, his throbbing heart and the chill along his back. Just a cloak and veil. Oh God! Until now, just a form, a shadow! And only last week he had been led into a similar hunt which turned out to be a shameful, fruitless venture. For a whole hour he had trotted behind a cloak and veil held by a white finger with a red manicured fingernail. Now, why would a cloak and veil deliberately exhibit a finger with a red fingernail if not . . . if not for the sole purpose of provocation? When you cover, you cover everything, or else what is the point? And if you manage to conceal the whole body, is it so hard to include a fingernail? Mischievous deceit was the motive. Heartless villainous fraud! A whole hour of maneuvering walks to end in the hustle of the wholesale market, the veiled figure mysteriously disappearing in the confusion of pedestrians, shoppers and loaded donkeys. In vain he had searched; in vain he had entered shops on stupid pretexts, the owners eyeing him suspiciously. The double loss! One hour in pursuit and another in search.

Suddenly anger flooded his entire being. He hated them both; the one with the red-manicured fingernail and the one with the dainty shoes and the two popping toes. What crumbs were they offering him? What claim had they? When he had only to close his eyes for his room to fill . . . to fill with such bountiful riches that he wouldn't be able to move without stumbling against marble breasts, serpentine legs and mountainous buttocks. A finger and a coquettish fingernail, a dainty shoe and two popping toes, indeed! He hated them both so much . . . he wished he could knock them down on a bed or a carpet. Was he forever to be fed on ephemeral repasts, mere shadows and apparitions? What else was there? Professional Rema at the end of a dark alley with hoodlums and criminals loitering at the corner?

Rema with the raucous voice and extravagant prices, her clownishly rouged girls with God knew what diseases? Should he switch back to following the respectable, unveiled Jewish girls, to encounter scorn, annoyance, even fear? But these were hopeless, pedestrian: nothing to conceal, so nothing to offer. Locked merchandise, sealed for marriage and marriage alone. And where was his own savior, purgatory marriage? Doomed to stand in line behind a bunch of older brothers and sisters, all at the threshold, all stumbling at the closed door. Keep fumbling in your pocket, merciful matchmaker, keep fumbling for the golden key.

Despair followed anger as the black cloak and veil sensuously floated along the streets of a well-to-do residential area. Again the forlorn beggars at the corners of two-story houses. Ah, the endless rows of windows! How many females peeping behind each pane?

Was he an incurable girl-chaser, an empty-handed, harmless offender, scorned by men and laughed at by women!

"Do you follow girls, Ovadia? A twenty-three-year-old like you?" The sister had chuckled and the mother had grinned behind her straw fan. How did they know, who told them? He had ignored chuckles and grins, but the memory of them never failed to produce that cold sweat. . . .

But what was this? The veil turning its head back, back toward its pursuer? Blessed be the dead, the living and the ones to be born! Was it a sign, a summons or, no, a plain mistake? The rhythmic, steady pace of the four feet went on, his, alert and watchful. What, again turning its head! No possible mistake this time! Come, wild imagination, fly up to the seventh sky, to the heaven of heavens. Throb, throb, heart, till you burst! Sweet chill, chill the back, chill it to death, for such death is ecstasy. And you weary, faithful legs, race away to the end of the world! The suddenly familiar street did not look familiar; it was sprinkled with roses and jasmines. Neither did the familiar wooden door; it was a golden gate with white birds sprawling about. Nor the black silk-embroidered veil, ceremoniously lifted up? No! But the grimacing face, oh yes! His cousin's! And the mocking words, oh God!

"Won't you come in, Ovadia?"

Again

"Fortune teller, fortune teller." The melodious call grew nearer, forecasting the coming of spring when peddlers roamed the streets.

Grandma's ears pricked up. "Esther," she called.

I raised my eyes. "You want me to call him, Grandma? Are you sure?"

"Of course I'm sure."

"Fortune teller, fortune teller," the call was close by now. "No God but Allah and Muhammad is his messenger."

I went to the door and peered into the narrow street. "Hey you, fortune teller!"

He turned his head and his eyes inspected the houses for the source of the call. Then he saw me and came over, his ragged cloak dangling.

"This way," I said and showed him into the house.

He stood by the edge of the piazza. "Allah be with you, aunt," he greeted my grandma while his eyes made the round of the old big house, its chipped arches and peeling paint, the row of room doors, some with locks, others just shut.

"Come into the piazza," Grandma said.

"Is it for her, aunt?" he asked, pointing at me.

"For her! Are you crazy, she is twelve years old."

The fortune teller turned his eyes toward the family picture on the side wall. It was large, black and white, with Grandma, her parents and siblings.

"Anyone else?" he asked.

"No one lives here, except me and the young girl," Grandma snapped.

"It is for you then?"

"Yes, it is for me."

He stepped into the piazza, tucked back his cloak and sat on the brick floor. He stretched his legs, spread them and his torn laceless shoes popped out from under his tunic. Grandma fetched a wooden stool and sat in front of him, her long shift hiding her small, frail limbs.

It was late in the day. The sun was up the wall at the end of the piazza and a light breeze rocked the lean branches of the lemon tree.

The fortune teller pushed back his soiled turban. He put his hands in his pockets and extracted a handful of cheap colored stones, blue, red and white. He held them up to Grandma for inspection, then he closed both hands on them. He shut his eyes, lifted his withered face and began reciting:

"In the name of Allah the merciful, Moussa [Moses], Issah [Jesus] and Muhammad . . . ," and the rest of the words were mumbled. Suddenly his hands opened, letting go of the stones which spread at random between his legs. He opened his eyes, and looked at them.

"Ah, ah," he exclaimed and bobbed his head a few times; then his face muscles relaxed and he turned to Grandma:

"Your stars are high above and your soul is of pure gold. The stream of shiny years is before you. Your heart is longing after someone but that someone's heart is after the wind." He stopped when he saw Grandma shake her head. "In the next ten days," he resumed and Grandma's gaze followed his words and the movement of his fingers, "someone, his name long forgotten, will bring you something valuable. Ah, and beware of the yellow color. Treacherous for you. Avoid it in dress, food and drink. Aha, there is someone, neither young nor old, neither tall nor short, whose evil eye is after you. Beware his shadow." And the fortune teller stopped to look at Grandma's puzzled stare. "Now," he began again. "If you give me an extra five fils, I will prepare you a bunch of small herbs which will guard you from this evil eye. You keep the herbs under your pillow, smell them every morning and they will lead you to everything that is good. Health, wealth, and happiness."

Grandma let out a long sigh and studied the fortune teller from head to foot. "If you were that good," she said, "you would have done better for yourself. Just look at you. Now say something more from the stones and that will be all."

He turned to look back at the stones. Then he began. "You have a bird, a white delicate bird . . . ," and Grandma listened with a smile on her face. When he finally finished, she turned to me:

"Bring him a glass of milk and a piece of bread."

I went into the kitchen, fetched the largest glass for milk, a big piece of bread and came back.

"May Allah bless you," he turned to me as he stretched his hand for the food. He drank and ate in silence, his eyes avoiding us.

Grandma stood up, tucked her hand into her slip's pocket and came out with the fee.

"No." He pushed back her hand. "In the name of your Moussa, the milk and bread are enough."

"No, you take it. Take it, I tell you."

He took his fee, stood up and headed for the door. "Allah be with you," he told Grandma and, pointing at me, he added, "May Allah keep her for you."

The next week, when he passed our door, his call did not sound loud. But Grandma's ears were on edge and I raised my eyes toward her.

"Are you sure, Grandma? Sure you want me to call him?"

"Yes, I am sure."

Their First Pogrom

"**M**ore and more are coming, Mother." Joe peered through the layers of the straw blind. "And all with home furniture."

"May they be blind and break their limbs. May they . . ." Habiba launched into a tirade of curses and turned sideways on her couch. "Looting homes! Unheard of!"

The "heard-of" for both Mother and son was the looting of stores: a single episode accompanying the British entry into Baghdad in 1918. Rumor had it that the British soldiers had inaugurated the event by obligingly firing at the store locks. It had been their idea of a little distraction for the populace, some compensation for the presence of a foreign army. The mob had gone wild, and the whole bazaar, Moslem, Christian and Jewish stores, was looted.

Twenty-three years had passed, twenty-three years of relative calm and prosperity. Even the one-month coup, a pro-Nazi regime, proved an advocate of law and order. "But now that the Regent is back," Joe went on muttering to himself, "now that the revolt is defeated, this. . . ." Definitely a pogrom. The first one. Joe watched a barefoot hoodlum hopping in his struggle with an armchair and two velvet cushions. A black-veiled peasant woman followed, a folded carpet arched across her back. Through the closed corner window, faint, distant screams were heard. Joe had abandoned the bewildering "why" and the murderous despair against man, the elements and God. Fear alone remained, fear which crept into his bones and sent chills through his chest. Just when everything was getting back to normal: the one-month coup totally defeated and the pro-British regime back at the outskirts of the city; just now, in the process of normalization, the junta finally ousted and the Jews able to breathe again, just when . . .

"Mother, they're attacking Ezra's house." Joe strained his eyes and his nose scraped the blind. A wave of hot-cold sweat passed through him. The early morning rumors, which he had not passed on to his mother, came back to him: more than looting was at stake, more than looting.

"Damned be their lot and scattered their entrails." Habiba sat up, her frail sixty-year-old body clad in a white tunic with a fringed gillet and lace underwear. Her feet fumbled for her slippers and she slowly stood up. "Come hide in the other room and let me handle it alone," she called to her son.

And whoever was familiar with the mentality of the time and place would agree that it was a necessary precaution. In any slippery situation, unless one had the upper hand, the presence of a man was hardly desirable. It was said to awaken the foul instincts which the presence of a woman lulls into deep sleep. More so an elderly woman, more so Habiba with her audacity and quick wit. So the mother led her forty-year-old son into the room, a rather small room with two brass beds, a dresser, boxes of clothes, trunks and piled bedding. She made him crawl into a straw carpet which she had rolled over and over to fit his heavy body. She pushed some bedding and boxes in front of the carpet, and then she saw his face.

"Don't worry!" she snapped. "Don't I know the dirty beggars? They'll take a few things; that's all. God's wrath upon them!"

Habiba went back into the living room, which was actually a hallway, its floor covered with an old wall-to-wall carpet. She again inspected the locks of the three steel trunks lined up against the back wall. A beige muslin cover with six striped brown cushions transformed the trunks into seats, while the one wooden couch served as a daybed for Habiba. The steel table and chairs stood under the two-columned arch separating the room from the piazza. Outside, the sun was halfway across the small garden with its single tree. Habiba checked the living room for any forgotten valuable that might be lying outside the trunks. Then she went to inspect the heavy table which Joe had set against the door with its big wooden latch. Satisfied to the extent that one could be satisfied under the circumstances, she returned to her couch, arranged the cushions, leaned back and waited. Her eyes wandered about the white stucco walls and settled on the one small decoration. It was a photograph of her grandparents, her parents and eight uncles and aunts. The grandparents sat in the middle while the others stood behind and to the sides. All were dressed in their best suits; all smiled gently. She rested her gaze on her thin veined hands. Soon the latch gave way, the door squealed, overturning the table, and Mustapha and his son leapt in front of her.

Mustapha had come all the way from Kurch Street. At about eleven in the morning he had been in his damp box-like store, bent over a leaking brass kettle. Suddenly his young wife, Latifa, barefoot and breathless, appeared at the threshold.

"They are looting the Jewish quarter of Samra!" she exclaimed. "They started early in the morning and you're the only one who didn't know."

"Looting? Are you sure?"

"Yes. Everybody is going. Shagab got a carpet. Come on, hurry up. Everybody is taking. Why not you?"

Mustapha stood up, his tall figure almost touching the ceiling. He looked at his sixteen-year-old boy hammering at a pot.

"He will stay in the store and I will go."

"No," she cried, "close the store and take him with you. You will have many things to carry. If it wasn't for the baby, I would come too."

"Oh, I want to come along," cried the lad.

Mustapha went for his cloak and shoes.

"You don't need them," Latifa called. "It's so hot and you won't have far to go. Hurry up."

Mustapha didn't answer. He put on his shoes and his cloak, closed the store and, accompanied by his son, hastened toward the Samra quarter. At the edge of Liyya Street, he encountered people carrying all kinds of household goods, ranging from expensive Persian carpets and mother-of-pearl tables to broken chairs and old garbage cans. They were hurrying, hurrying to unload and return for more. The boy questioned some looters, and they pointed out an area two streets below. Arriving there, Mustapha and his son saw a crowd of twenty people, men and women, three or four of them busy forcing a door. Mustapha skipped four houses in order to be on his own, and his choice fell on Joe's house.

"It is a shame. I have nothing to break the door with."

"I brought the hammer with me." The son produced the tool from the pocket of his tunic.

With the hammer, the strength and determination of the two men, it was a matter of minutes before the door gave way and Mustapha and his son were inside the sunny open-air courtyard.

Mustapha's swift glance made note of the living room and the woman. Followed by his son, he quickly peered through the other rooms, the kitchen and the bathroom. Finding no one, he came back into the living room and without a word concentrated on the three trunks. He swept away the cushions and blankets and, uncovering the thick heavy locks, frantically pulled and pushed at them.

Habiba at first ignored the two men and kept her eyes on the door, waiting for others. When none showed up, she stood and walked toward Mustapha.

"All three are locked," exclaimed Mustapha. "Woman, give me the keys."

"You shout at me and I could be old enough to be your mother. Shame on you! To frighten a woman, a big man like you with such a long mustache."

Mustapha did not answer. One hand went to his mustache and the other kept plucking at the locks.

She waited for an answer, and when none came, her voice rose sharply. "A woman living alone! Have you no fear of God?" The word God sent a sharp sting into Mustapha's chest. Ominous lines from the Koran hammered in his ears and shook him to distraction while his hands kept clutching at the locks.

"Where are the keys, aunt?" he asked.

"The trunks belong to my daughter." She stared at Mustapha's handsome features and his tall strong body. "The keys are with her and she left for Basra. Good she did not stay to see such a day! No fear of God, no pity, the end of the world!"

Mustapha left the trunks and went to the dresser. He pulled open drawer after drawer as piles of women's clothes drifted to the floor. Then the carpet caught his eyes. He motioned to his son and they both proceeded to move the trunks, the couch and the dresser.

She watched him, a robust forty-five-year-old man with swift movements. "Have you no heart, no pity? Am I to spend the chilly winter with the cold brick floor under my feet?"

Mustapha stopped. His eyes wandered about the place while he reluctantly dropped the carpet and hurried to the kitchen with Habiba at his heels. Her body brushed the ends of his thick brown cloak and the rough material scratched her bare arm. He went for the kettle and turned it over in his hands, his professional eye noting the quality of the brass.

"Now, how am I to make tea if you take away my kettle?"

He put down the kettle and returned to the living room, to lift the two duck-feather sleeping cushions.

"My breath is so heavy even the two cushions are not enough."

He let go of the cushions and turned toward Habiba.

"Shall I take the trunk cushions and the tablecloth?"

"Take them if it makes you happy," she sighed.

He gathered up the cushions and the tablecloth and was about to plunge his hands inside the open dresser drawers when suddenly he hesitated, looked at Habiba and decided against it. "God be with you," he said and, without waiting for an answer, hurried outside and closed the door, pulling the table as close to its original position as he could possibly manage.

Outside, he was about to return home when his son vehemently urged him to go on.

"We must try for more," the boy said, scowling.

Mustapha agreed, suggesting they enter an already forced house. As he was about to do so, some frightened looters came running down the streets, some carrying their loot, some dropping it in the street.

"The police are coming with rifles," they announced.

"So what, the police themselves . . ." Mustapha's son began.

"Not anymore. They mean business now."

And Mustapha and his son, joining the looters, took to their heels.

It was estimated that three hundred Jews were killed during the pogrom: three hundred men, women and children. The Jewish community was consumed with questions and answers. What had happened to the God-fearing Arab and his Koran's tolerance? Was the new killer of women and children the same chivalrous Arab? What had happened to a reasonably good relationship? Was it a distraction planned by the entering army? Was it the effect of the Nazi propaganda? Was it . . . ? Jewish young men kept away from the night clubs, and Jewish women deserted the clothing shops. None rode boats along the river; none sat on the benches facing the water or strolled along the shore. They gathered in homes, synagogues, and endlessly discussed the pogrom. There were eyewitness accounts; in the streets, unsuspecting men had been seized and beaten to death; others had been slaughtered in their looted homes; some had been zealously protected by Arab neighbors, others by kindly passersby; the episode of Habiba was treated as a joke.

"How come you were not afraid?" she was teased.

"Why should I be?"

"You are really something."

But anxious voices were less favorable. "You should have given them whatever they wanted. You took your life in your hands." Habiba shrugged disdainfully and went on repeating her story. But details of the pogrom poured in, forcing her to face the atrocities. She visualized Mustapha's heavy body and his murderous goyish eyes. The voices persisted: "These are not the Arabs that you know. You shouldn't have pushed your luck." Finally Habiba sighed and conceded:

"It was my first pogrom. I didn't know."

Inside her house, Latifa spurned Mustapha's loot while her son related the details of their adventure.

"Is that so?" Latifa scowled. "You! You should have seen what Ismail brought."

"She was a woman. An elderly woman."

"You should hear what the others did."

"Shut up, woman."

"Who knows what was there in those trunks? We could have forced her . . . ," the son put in.

"You too shut up or you'll get it."

Latifa and her son did shut up, but they told the story to everyone: brothers, cousins, neighbors . . . and Mustapha was besieged by ridicule:

"Tell us about the old woman, Mustapha."

"It is good you hadn't taken off your underwear and given it to her."

The teasing became irritable; Jews had gone out to greet the old returning regime, the "lackey government." They were a shrewd, lousy bunch, getting rich at the expense of others. In the West, that clever world with all the answers, they knew how to deal with them. In Russia, they treated them with pogroms; in Germany they killed them in concentration camps. It was only the Arabs who were meek. The teasing grew insistent, its arguments convincing, and Mustapha, fists clenched, finally made his pledge:

"It was my first pogrom. I didn't know. Next time . . ."

Forbidden Correspondence

Ephraim's hands shook as he held the two letters, then the ominous implications took shape. Would he be arrested and sent to prison, would he be tortured and end up. . . . Would a bribe suffice? How much?

He shuffled past the kitchen and watched his mother's back, her silvery head bent over the dirty dishes in the sink. Should he ask her advice? She might well give him a suggestion? No, he would not burden her with his predicament. She had become quite edgy since his siblings, Rebecca and Shlomo, had emigrated to Israel while she remained alone with him and his twelve-year-old brother Sami. Though Israel had won its War of Independence, skirmishes with the Arabs had not ceased, and his mother was constantly worried.

He headed toward the hallway, turned on the light and sat down, trying to remain calm; he knew that nervousness was not healthy for him; it usually triggered an asthma attack.

Again he looked at the letters. The one from the CID—Central Intelligence Department—gave no hint as to the seriousness of his situation. It just stated that he should appear within five days from the day the letter was posted. The second letter was from Rebecca, dated

41

1947, long before Israel was declared a state, long before Zionism was decreed a crime against this state, punishable by death. And all that it said was that Rebecca missed the family and she had just started working in an accounting firm. Nothing except the longing of a young girl for the warmth of her family and her anxiety over tackling her first job. Anyway, it was not he who had sent the letter, it was not he who had corresponded with the enemy. Let them go after Rebecca if they could. He actually should not worry. He had never studied Hebrew with the underground Zionist organization; he had never tried crossing the border and been caught; he had no Moslem friend or acquaintance who could suddenly turn nasty and make false accusations against him. Some Moslems did, out of enmity or plain meanness.

Should he consult a lawyer or . . . ? And suddenly he remembered Jamil, Shlomo's friend. Jamil had connections with influential Moslems, with the heads of the CID, and he often helped his fellow Jews in awkward situations. It was Jamil who arranged first Rebecca's and then Shlomo's illegal emigration to Israel.

The thought of Jamil as a go-between on his behalf eased his heartbeat. He stood up and walked to the back porch. He needed some fresh air to cool his head. There was none, though. The moonless evening was hot and breezeless. Baghdad's June was no bargain. He took a deep breath and the exotic smell of the Jasmine branch filled his nostrils. Then he sat in the dim light of the porch and again reviewed the letters; again weighed his predicament.

He might as well call Jamil right there and then; the earlier to ease his tension the better. And it was only seven-thirty. He shuffled inside, took the phone book, looked up the number and dialed.

A gentle feminine voice answered the ring. "Hello."

"Can I speak with Jamil, please?"

"Just a second."

It must be the wife and he was glad she did not ask who he was. His impatience was . . .

"Hello. This is Jamil."

"Good evening. I am the brother of Shlomo Kabaza. And I have a problem. Could you help me, please?"

"I believe I know the nature of your problem. But right now I am out of contact."

"My problem is urgent and . . ."

"Can't you deal with it yourself? Haven't you ever been in a similar situation?"

"No."

There was a moment of silence. Then came Jamil's subdued voice: "I can only give you some advice. Meet me tomorrow. . . ."

"Would you please make it tonight?" Ephraim could hear the supplication in his voice.

Again a moment of silence. Then Jamil said, "I have some business to deal with right now. I can only see you at nine tonight. Do you want to meet me at Café BaBa then?"

"Oh yes, and thank you so much."

"My pleasure."

Ephraim walked the two blocks to the main street along the Dejla shore and waited for a coach. Soon one came by. He bargained the price with the coachman and got in.

The coach drove along the river shore. It was dark and the few street lights cast a dim shadow on the water. Some transportation boats docked along the water's edge. Hardly any pedestrians on the sidewalk. It was a Jewish neighborhood with the beautiful two-story villas along the shore. Not a soul on the balconies either. He recalled the days when the street swarmed with Jews strolling along, sitting on the benches or taking a river-boat ride. He recalled an incident when one Jewish girl was leaning on her balcony and a Moslem young man, passing by, called, "Oh God, let me be a railing." Then he remembered the pogrom eight years earlier when Moslem young men stood in the neighboring streets and discussed which Jewish girl would be for which one of them. Their wishes did not materialize because the pogrom stopped short of the wealthy Jewish neighborhood. What befell the poor Jewish girls in the slums, he did not know.

Suddenly his chest constricted. What lay in store for him? The thought of his brother Shlomo being gone filled him with sadness and anger. Shlomo knew how to deal with difficulties. Shouldn't he be here to help with the situation? The first time Shlomo tried to cross the border to Jordan, he was caught, jailed and fined. It didn't stop him from trying again. In vain Mother argued that it was not the right time, that the Jews and Arabs of Palestine were still fighting, and that the Iraqi government would finally give passports to the Jews. "How long would they keep us hostages?" She would say. "And you have a good job and some good Moslem friends." And immediately Shlomo responded with a lecture: "I don't know how long they will keep us hostages. And how does it help me to have some good Moslem friends? I still walk the street looking behind me. And the government is gradually dismissing all Jewish clerks. How long do you think I can keep my job? Also . . ."

Mother could not venture to argue with Rebecca; Rebecca was a fully commited Zionist, and she left before Israel was declared a state. As for himself, Mother had only a few words: "Life is hard in Palestine, while you have a good accounting job here. Then there is your asthma." He knew he had his asthma. Did she have to remind him all the time?

Ephraim believed that what caused Shlomo to insist on leaving was an embarrassing and scary incident a few months before he left. Shlomo had become friendly with a young girl he had met at the gym of a Jewish school. The place had a tennis court which was available to outsiders after school hours, and young people made good use of it. One early evening after their tennis game, Shlomo and the young girl went for a walk in a newly built promenade. It was a wide street with eucalyptus trees along the sidewalks, flower beds and palm trees in the middle. Suddenly a whistle blew right behind Shlomo and the girl, and they turned to see a man wearing a Moslem kaffiya sneering at them. Shlomo took the girl by the hand and began to run. The man ran after them. Fortunately, a few people suddenly came out from a side street. Shlomo and the girl stuck to them and the man gradually took off. "I could have given it to him," Shlomo had told Ephraim. "He was not even that young, but I ran like a mouse. You know how it is with us Jews." And Ephraim knew how it was. If a Jew and a Moslem fought in the street, the few Jewish passersby would run off fearing for their lives, while a crowd of Moslems gathered, out of nowhere, to join the fight on their brother's behalf. As for a Jew going to the police, it was a waste of time at best.

Ephraim reached the Jewish Café Baba at five to nine. The place was empty except for two men sitting by a table at the end of the café. They seemed engaged in a heated conversation, but Ephraim could not make out what they were saying. Soon the waiter with the white apron came over and asked Ephraim what he wished to order.

"I am waiting for a friend," Ephraim said and at that very moment Jamil arrived and walked over to Ephraim. "You look very much like your brother, Shlomo."

Ephraim nodded.

"It's a letter, isn't it?" Jamil asked.

"Yes, how did you know?"

"You aren't the only one. These are old letters, sent by Iraqi Jews in Israel to their relatives here. The British in Palestine didn't send them on time and now, as they vacated the land, they decided to deliver them into the hands of our CID. Why, we don't know."

"Should I hire a lawyer?"

"Oh, no." Jamil shook his head. "A lawyer would make matters worse. It should be settled by a bribe. You just bribe the officer in charge."

"I don't know who he is."

"Anyone who will deal with your case."

"But they will say I am bribing a police officer, a crime . . ."

"No, they won't." Jamil shook his head.

Ephraim remained confused.

"I tell you they won't," Jamil repeated. "And you are talking to someone who has dealt with these matters for a long time now. I would have taken care of it myself, except that right now I'm asking a big favor from a head captain at the CID. It's a serious matter, not like yours. So I don't want to jeopardize the situation."

Ephraim felt comforted that Jamil did not consider his case to be serious.

"But how should I go about it? Right away I tell him I am giving him a bribe?"

"You'll be wearing a jacket, no? So put your hand inside the pocket of your jacket and he will understand."

"And how much should I give him?"

"Twenty dinars should be enough. And deal with it tomorrow, the earlier the better."

The waiter with the white apron approached again. And both Ephraim and Jamil ordered tea with cardamom.

Ephraim suddenly remembered that he had not yet thanked Jamil. "It is so nice of you to have come at such short notice," he said.

"No problem."

"I know that you have connections and you help a lot. Shlomo told me about you."

Jamil nodded and sipped his tea.

"And frankly I was so worried," Ephraim continued. "When you hear all the incitement against the Jews on the radio and the newspaper. . . ."

"Are you telling me?" Jamil sighed.

"Do you think it will get any better?"

Jamil gave Ephraim a look, more of a stare than a look. It was obvious that he did not want to comment.

"Some think it would get worse," Ephraim went on.

"Whatever happens, happens. We go day by day."

"So few people at the café." Ephraim changed the subject.

"These are hard days for us Jews."

Suddenly Jamil gulped his remaining tea and stood up. "Sorry, I have to leave. I have many things to do. But don't worry. It isn't a serious matter. You'll see." Jamil put his hand in his pants' pocket and extracted his purse.

"No, no," Ephraim vehemently objected.

"All, right."

"And thank you again for coming, and for the advice."

"You're welcome. And again, don't worry."

Now alone, Ephraim thought about going home; then suddenly he decided to order some arak. Some arak to enliven his spirits. He called to the waiter and leaned back in his chair.

Ephraim woke with a start, remembering what lay in store for him. Actually he had slept quite well. Last night's arak had had its effect, especially since he was not a drinker. He remembered how worried he had been when he first saw the letters and how Jamil had calmed him down. Jamil knew what he was talking about. Twenty dinars were more than half Ephraim's monthly salary, but he would not bargain; he just wanted the whole thing to be over, so he could finally relax. He picked up the phone and informed Jacob, his colleague at work, that he would be late or might even take the whole day off, depending on the outcome of a certain matter.

The police headquarters would be open at eight, but he would not go that early. He didn't care to be the officers' first target of the day; their animosity would be at its height. Who knew what was best and what was worst? Nine o'clock would be fine, neither here nor there.

It took ages for the clock to reach eight-thirty so that Ephraim could set out for the police station. And as the time approached he became more and more nervous. What if the officer refused the bribe, what if it made him angry? He should be very tactful. There was a rumor that bribes were no longer that effective. No wonder, with all the incitement on the government-controlled radio and in the newspapers: the Jews were the worst people in the world, and not just the Zionists, the Jews in general.

It was an old, large two-story building with four big columns, the Iraqi flag fluttering over its second floor. Ephraim passed by the policeman at the door, who eyed him menacingly. Inside, his eyes raced over the narrow corridor filled with policemen, until he spotted the information booth. He approached with the letter, and the clerk pointed at a room to the right.

"Just knock on the door," the clerk said.

Ephraim could hardly hear his knock. But he clearly heard the sharp, "Come in."

He entered and faced an officer sitting behind a large desk. The officer was in his thirties, dark, with large features. He was frowning, his thick black eyebrows curved downward.

"Now what do we have here?" the officer sneered.

Ephraim extended the two letters and the officer took them.

"Officer . . ." Ephraim began.

"Don't I know how to read?" the officer snapped and gave Ephraim a harsh look.

Ephraim felt his hand shaking.

"Hm," the officer said without taking his eyes off the letters. "This is serious. Corresponding with the enemy." He finally looked Ephraim in the face.

Ephraim's hand awkwardly neared his jacket; he was sure that the officer noted the movement.

"Maybe we can work out something." The officer spoke slowly, and turned back to the letters.

Ephraim relaxed and his hand fell from his chest. He should be tactful. He would give the bribe later, saying it was just a way of thanking him.

The officer looked up and eyed Ephraim. "I'm afraid it's a very serious matter, too serious."

Ephraim's heart began to gallop and his hand rushed inside his jacket.

"But I will see what I can do."

Ephraim relaxed and his hand fell from his jacket again. He must be careful about the bribe.

"Now why do you people have to correspond with the enemy?" The officer's tone turned harsh and immediately Ephraim's hand, once again, quickly moved to his jacket.

"Give, give, even your God is taking bribes." Exasperation was all over the officer's face. Ephraim extracted the envelope with the money and handed it to the officer.

The officer began counting, his expression relaxed. He put the money in his drawer, then reached for the letters.

"Officer," Ephraim began awkwardly, "my sister left . . ."

The officer stopped Ephraim with a wave of his hand.

"Now who says you have a sister?" the officer began, a contemptuous sneer on his face, while he took the two letters, tore them to pieces and threw them in a nearby wastebasket.

"Go, go now, go home to your mother," The officer made a dismissive wave of his hand, contempt still on his face.

"Thank you, sir." Ephraim breathed hard and hurried out the door; he hurried even faster through the corridor and was finally outside. Out to freedom, sweet freedom. He would go to a nearby café and order a delicious cup of orange juice, then tea, then. . . . He had planned on going back to work as soon as he finished with the CID, but no; he would take the whole day off. It annoyed him that the officer told him "Go to your mother," not "Go to your wife." Did he look that young? Twenty-five was not too young to have a wife. Was it his obvious fear that made him look pitiful? Would Shlomo have handled it differently? And what if he had? Who cared whether he, Ephraim, was timid or brave? He was free, free. He smiled thinking about God taking bribes. From whom? Who would dare. . . . Oh, how he wished to bribe God! For what was in store, in store for the future. . . .

The Flesh Bubble

Dr. Gabbai turned the electric fan up to its highest level. He went over to the sink, opened the faucet and threw some water on his face. August was the hottest month in Baghdad. He pulled a small towel from the nearby rack and patted his face. Soon he heard the faint knock at the door, put back the towel and called, "Come in."

His assistant directed a man and a woman into the room.

"Good morning, doctor, Abed Ilam, your servant," the man said as he entered. He looked to be about forty-five. His dark face was dominated by thick eyebrows and large, black, sinister eyes. He wore a white tunic and a brown cloak and his head was covered with the white black-dotted Moslem kaffiya. The woman was clad in a black cloak and veil, covered from head to foot, nothing showing. She was obviously not a working woman or a peddler or anything like that, otherwise she would need to bare her face or at least her eyes. She could afford to be covered all over.

The man sat on one of the chairs and the woman sat on the floor.

"Why on the floor?" Gabbai said. "Here is another chair."

"No," the man said and made a restraining gesture with his hand. "A woman. She sits on the floor."

Moslem men! Gabbai thought. Good for them. Let our Jewish women come and watch. Nothing was enough for them and their latest refrain: absolute equality in Israel; men and women treated exactly the same.

"What's the problem?" Gabbai asked.

"The wife. She is sick," the man answered.

"What is she suffering from?"

"You're the doctor, you should know."

Gabbai remained silent for a moment. He knew the people he was dealing with. This was the village of Zura, not Baghdad. But even Baghdad. . . .

"Give her an injection, doctor. A good one," the man said.

Oh, how they love injections! They would settle for medicine, but injections were the ultimate goal.

Gabbai decided on a B12. He remembered his early days as a doctor in the village when he insisted on practicing real medicine and how he gradually came to accept his patient's eccentricities. But a B12 could not possibly hurt. He prepared the syringe and stood ready.

The man had directed his wife to the examining table and pulled her up. Then he began to struggle with her clothes to provide the tiny space for the injection without revealing the rest of her body. Gabbai had turned away his face to allow the man some privacy in his maneuvering.

"Ready," the man finally said.

Gabbai proceeded toward the tiny circle of flesh. It was olive-colored, smooth and soft, and the man was holding the black cloth around it. In a quick flash, Gabbai inserted the needle, followed by the loud, painful cry of pain, then gently administered the piece of cotton. He held it for a while, then put on a small plastic bandage.

The man helped the woman off the examining table and she again sat on the floor.

"Thank you, doctor," the man said. "How much?"

"One dinar for the visit, and a quarter for the injection."

The man deposited the money on an end table. "God be with you, doctor," he said, and left the room followed by his wife.

Gabbai suddenly felt tired. No wonder, it was almost noon. And the heat! He decided on a break and informed his assistant. The patients could wait. He sat on his reclining wooden chair, pulled his legs up and closed his eyes. He thought of the woman's round spot of flesh where he had made his injection. He thought of his wife, Seraphine. What a complainer! Sometimes he felt like slapping her face. But Jewish men wouldn't hit their wives. At least not the men in his class, the lower middle class and up. "If a man loves his wife, God will bestow on him; If a man cheats on his wife, something bad would befall his children." Some nonsense in the Talmud to keep the men in check while the women. . . . And he loved his children. He had married Seraphine when he was twenty-six years old, quite young compared to how late Jewish men married in Baghdad. Her family promised, aside from the dowry, to get him into medical school, which they did. These were the late forties; even the quota of two Jewish admissions a year was no longer granted. But Seraphine's brothers had powerful Moslem friends, partners in an export firm. The brothers themselves were like Moslems. Tough and loud-mouthed. Seraphine was plain, maybe on the pretty side. Except that after having Ezra and Mathilda, she became quite fat. And such a complainer! He never confronted her. He just sulked and that made her complain even more. Sometimes he wished he could hit her in the mouth, but . . .

He felt like dozing. He could use a nap. His eyes were heavy, yet he could see that Moslem woman's tiny round piece of flesh, smooth and soft. He caressed it gently and the touch was so cool it sent a shiver through his loins. Then he noticed that the piece of flesh was inflating and growing bigger. It grew bigger by the minute and he had a bad premonition. He was suddenly afraid. The piece of flesh turned into a bubble as big as a cantaloupe, smooth and soft. He withdrew his hand when the bubble suddenly burst and he emitted a cry of fear. He opened his eyes and looked around. Did he really cry out or was it just in the dream? But he recovered from his fright and smiled to himself.

* * *

Gabbai saw Abed Ilam and his wife waiting among the patients. He smiled as he remembered the bubble and his own dream. And he waited. He waited for Abed Ilam to come into his office.

Finally Abed Ilam entered in with the wife behind him. He sat on the chair and the wife sat on the floor. Gabbai did not object this time.

"Good morning, doctor. Your servant Abed Ilam."

"So what is it today, the same problem as last time?"

"What last time?" Abed Ilam looked perplexed.

"Didn't you come to me three months ago when the woman was sick?"

"Oh, this is a different one. The other turned out to be trash. I returned her to her people. She was trash."

The man must have means to afford a second dowry. But why didn't he keep both women? Moslem men are allowed more than one wife. Maybe she was a high consumer of food. Seraphine didn't eat that much. He shook his head at the absurdity of his thought. Food expense indeed. Such a trifle in his household.

The familiar procedure began: the man leading the wife to the examination table and the struggle with the clothes to find the small space among the black garments.

Gabbai saw the tiny piece of flesh, and it was neither soft nor smooth. Ragged and peeling as though sunburnt. Sunburnt indeed. Did she lie naked in the sun to get a tan? It was the residue of a rash. He absently prepared the needle, stuck it in, and as absently watched the man paying, the couple heading toward the door and finally leaving.

He felt like leaving the office and going home. Going home to . . . Seraphine?

Farewell to Dejla

I walked under the shade of palm trees, along the shore of the Dejla
River. The sun was setting and a faint glow of grayish pink filled
the sky. Soon the air would cool. Baghdad's April was mild, the evenings breezy with the fragrance of citron blossoms. Then I saw him,
walking in the opposite direction. The same skinny, tall figure, the
same straight hurried gait.

"Why do you always hurry?" my mother would ask him. "What is
there waiting for you?"

"Nothing." He would shake his head, thoughtful and somber.

True, not much awaited him. In his fifties, celibate, with no immediate family except for a brother, far off in Basra.

He saw me and slowed down. A smile hovered over his pleasant
features. He wore khaki shorts and shirt, black sandals too big for his
feet, its soles worn.

"How are you, Shimon?" I asked.

"All right, considering," he said and his hand went up to smooth
his grey hair.

"Considering." I nodded.

"I registered for the laissez-passer and all my savings were in the bank." He sighed. "Two thousand dinars. Gone, frozen by the government. But Israel will compensate."

I nodded again.

That laissez-passer, 1951, the first way out for Iraqi Jews after years of no passports, no exit visas, with persecution raging on. But there was a hitch. Jews who chose the laissez-passer had to forfeit their Iraqi nationality and leave for Israel only.

"What about you?" Shimon asked.

"No money in the bank. But we didn't sell the house. Prices had tumbled and my father decided to wait. He couldn't imagine the government would come up with the freeze since it didn't interfere with the early registration for the laissez-passer."

"Don't worry," Shimon said. "Israel will compensate. If you lose a house, you get one there. Money, you get the same amount."

I nodded again.

"And where are you heading?" he asked. "A young girl like you. Soon it will be dark and few people on the street, as you can see. Times are not the best."

"I am saying farewell to Dejla River."

"On the rivers of Babylon, there we sat and cried, remembering Zion," he chanted.

"No more shall I cry remembering Zion. I am going to see it tomorrow. My three-year-old new Zion."

"Oh, really."

"Yes, what about you?"

"My name did not come up yet."

"Well, I registered early for the laissez-passer."

"Good trip."

"The same to you."

I resumed my walk. A few sparrows seemed to join me, hopping from one palm tree to the next. I passed by the beautiful Jewish villas along the shore. Did their owners leave way before, when passports were still available for Jews? Or did they register for the laissez-passer? Perhaps they're staying, hoping for better times.

The fragrance of gardenia-jasmine hit my nostrils. I took a deep breath, slowed down and lingered close to the aromatic source. The sudden barking of a dog startled me. I crossed the street to the shadeless sidewalk along the water, and sat on one of the benches. Down the rampart, the river flow was smooth and serene, a shining glory under the fading sun.

I thought about Shimon and his two thousand dinars. How did he gather them? From the meager fees of those Torah lessons he gave to the children of the well-to-do and the wealthy? He went from house to house, offering his knowledge and expertise. The mothers would give him something to eat, to wear as well, judging from his usual loose clothes and sandals too big for his feet. My parents hired him to teach me and my two brothers the Torah, and I would say he did a good job. He would read the text, dig deep into its meaning and explain it to us. It pleased him when we responded and upset him when we didn't, which prompted my mother's reprimand. "Don't disappoint the man. He's a good teacher."

After going over a chapter with us, Shimon would then sing it, his melodious, mournful voice resounding through the house, emanating a sense of piety and love for the Torah. I remember my brothers and I humming the text long after he left.

So he had amassed two thousand dinars. The long years of toll and privation, to save for a black day. Israel would give him back the two thousand.

I dug into my bag and extracted the bottle and the paper for the inscription. What should I write? A meaningful message; a profound thought or a poetic similitude that would shake the soul of whomever read it. I would insert the inscription into the bottle, close it tight and throw it into the water. Pathetic romanticism, modeled on the story of a young girl who sent a message in a bottle and floated it into the river. As it happened, a Prince Charming found the bottle and read the message. He conducted a thorough search, found the young girl, married her, and they lived happily ever after. Some barefoot hoodlum would pick up my bottle, spurn the contents and throw it back into the river.

Down the rampart the Moslem boatmen awaited customers who needed to reach the opposite shore. What if I take a ride, my last day in Baghdad? The sun was just a streak of pink behind the far-off horizon, but there was still some time before dark. Just half-an-hour ride. If my parents were to see me now! There was one old, harmless-looking boatman, hanging about. I hurried down the rampart, looked around, and approached him. "I want to take a ride along the river."

"Where to?" he asked.

"Nowhere. Just half-an-hour ride."

"Twelve fils," he said.

"No, that's too much."

"It's evening, miss, and soon there will be customers."

"No," I said, glad to back out because of the price, and not from fear of a daring adventure.

"Wait, miss," he called, as he saw me walking away. "Ten fils, and it's a very good price, believe me."

I reluctantly walked back. "All right," I said.

He pulled the boat close to the shore and I hopped in. Then he stationed himself in front of me and reached for the oars. He looked to be in his seventies, his unshaven face dark and wrinkled. His white tunic, cloak and kaffiya were worn. I noticed that his shoes were torn near the toes.

"I will take you as far as the other shore and also by the bridge. It doesn't matter if it takes more than half an hour."

"Thank you," I said.

My last trip on Dejla, maybe not, who knows? Would time rekindle a craving for the birthplace, the childhood memories, pain and suffering forgotten or forgiven? For now it looks as though it will be my last. And yet, all I feel is ambivalence. Did those last years of persecution dull all my emotions? What about the dilemma of the laissez-passer, then the preparations for the emigration, then my parents' distress over the loss of our house? Would Israel really compensate? Reliable sources confirm that it will. For now I am simply taking a ride on a river, with a stranger boatman, the weather accommodatingly pleasant.

We advanced and turned sideways toward the bridge. A light breeze began rocking the boat. I put my hand into the water, took a handful and threw it on my face. They came back to me, those hot summer days learning to swim with my brothers. A little girl of nine then, I would skirt the shores, the cool water and gentle waves floating me around. "You have become a good swimmer," the instructor would say, then turn to my brothers. "Better than you two."

They did not last long, my swimming days. "Girls should not swim in the river," the rabbi had said. "It is not in line with Moslem customs." And my parents readily acquiesced.

I leaned back and took a deep breath.

"Dejla is beautiful, no?" The boatman smiled.

"Dejla is treacherous," I blurted. What a challenging comment! Why antagonize the man, why look for trouble? He knows I am Jewish, my looks and my dress.

He remained silent, then he ventured. "On account of the swirls?" he asked.

"Yes." The swirls that would suddenly catch an unaware swimmer and spin him down to doomsday, all desperate efforts to no avail. And the swirls were everywhere and nowhere.

"They say there is a way to locate them, then the government would put signs to warn people," he said.

"Maybe." I wanted to sound agreeable. The government, really! The government was good at harassing the Jews, not at developing the country.

"That building over there, it's the prison isn't it?" I asked.

"Yes."

The prison that tortured dozens of Jewish young men and women, on one pretext or another. Maybe I should write something about it and squeeze it into the bottle. I reached into my bag.

"There is the Jasra," the boatman said. "We are nearing it."

The Jasra, a small bare island that popped up every summer when the level of Dejla receded. My father's favorite place, his escape from the city's heat. He would take us there on moonlit nights and we would picnic and swim, the waters slightly warm, the air cool and dry. There would be other Jewish families partying, and we mingled. When animosities against the Jews intensified, we remained the only family going there; my father would not give up the island. We would be alone there, shattering the dark stillness. But then my mother insisted that it was too dangerous, and my father had to give in.

"Can we linger for a few minutes?" I asked the boatman.

"Yes, yes," he said.

He slowed the boat and I stood facing the small piece of bare land. I inhaled the air that divulged nothing except the smell of water and wet earth.

I took the bottle and piece of paper from my handbag. I hesitated, then wrote "Farewell to Dejla." Nothing with profound meaning or poetic resonance. Just plain "Farewell to Dejla." I inserted the paper into the bottle, closed it tight and threw it into the water.

The man watched me in silence.

Soon we were heading back, and the light began to dim.

"Nice days are coming, you should take more rides," the boatman said. "I will always give you a good price."

"It's my last day in Baghdad. Tomorrow I'm leaving."

He nodded and was silent. Then he ventured, "I know. So many Jews are leaving. It's a shame. The economy is dead. There is no work around. You see all these boatmen standing there, waiting for customers who aren't coming."

I nodded. For the rest of the trip he remained silent and so did I.

What was there to say?

He anchored the boat and tied the rope. I took out ten fils and presented it to him.

"No miss, no."

"Yes, what do you mean, no? It's your fee. You . . ."

"It's your last trip on Dejla, miss."

"No." I pushed the money into his hand.

"In the name of the prophet I won't take it. In the name of the prophet Abass I won't take it."

He would not take it, once he swore by the name of Abass.

"Go, miss, and may God go with you."

"Thank you," I mumbled and, head low, climbed the rampart toward the street. Suddenly I turned around and waved. The boatman was nowhere too be seen. I waved some more, but could not see him. I headed home. Home.

II: Iraqi Jews in Israel

The Melting Pot

A land of milk and honey
(The Torah/Deuteronomy, chapter 27, verse 7)

A land eating its inhabitants
(The Torah/Numbers, chapter 13, verse 32)

They were the years 1951 and 1952; the years of food rationing and first elections; the years an uprooted community—a hundred thousand people—stood, its heart raked with hope, regret and despair. Baghdad and Tel Aviv were 600 miles apart, a mere two-hour flight. But they were the opposite extremities of the world: East and West that would never meet.

"They did meet! At our expense!" cried the Iraqi immigrant community. "We were sold out, sold out like sheep. Ten dinars a head. Ben Gurion made the transaction with El-Said."

"Do they want their Israel?" Iraqi prime minister El-Said had mocked in a private conversation. "Let them have it. Let them go and sell grains. We will see how they like it. And who needs them? A nationalistic movement? You find them in the lead. A communist underground? They are at the root. Let them go. We also need some rest."

Noga, a new building project in Givatime, was a microcosm of the bewildered, uprooted Iraqi community. Twelve immigrant families had found refuge there. The project consisted of three four-story apartment houses in the shape of a three-sided square with a community courtyard in the middle. Though for the most part inhabited, the apartment houses were not completely finished, and piles of sand and bricks lay scattered randomly around the courtyard. The bricks often served as seats for the members of the immigrant community. Every afternoon, as the sun moved to the west and the gentle breezes wafted through the open lobbies, the immigrants would emerge one after the other, gather in the main lobby and begin their daily litany of nostalgia, dilemma and frustration.

"We were fed a heap of propaganda." Mrs. Dallal adjusted a folding chair she had brought from her apartment.

"True, true," Mr. Sasson agreed.

"Not really," Mr. Zilka said. "We knew it would be a hard life."

"We knew there would be food rationing and all that," Mrs. Dallal's voice rose sharply. "But we didn't know we would have to stand in line two hours for a miserable half kilo of onions. And two hours to catch the bus. At this rate our whole life will be spent standing in line. And the discrimination!"

Mr. Zilka moved uneasily in his chair, that was too small for his tall, well-built body. "Patience," he said, "it will get better."

"Two liras for a broom, a whole day's salary," Mr. Sasson complained. "And the Arabs kept warning us: 'Life is too hard in Palestine. It's not for you.' But who would listen? Do you know that my neighbor wept when he left us? They weren't bad, these Arabs."

"Have you forgotten the 1941 pogrom?" Mr. Zilka asked.

"That was the work of the British."

"And the bomb at the Alwya club? . . . Life is hard in Israel. But what choice did they leave us? Harassment and persecution and no passports to Jews for five to six years. And suddenly they come up with the laissez-passer where we could leave if we gave up our Iraqi nationality. Shouldn't we have grabbed it?"

"No," Mr. Sasson said. "Those who stayed might be allowed regular passports; they might be able to sell their assets and leave for wherever they want—England, America. . . . And they could take everything with them. Not like us, with only a bundle of clothes on our back, all our things confiscated by the Iraqi government."

"At the airport my son tried to sneak in his tennis racket, his Parker pen and some family snapshots," Mr. Zilka said. "They took away everything."

"You were the enemy," Mr. Sasson replied. "They gave you a choice. And you chose the laissez-passer to Israel rather than retain your Iraqi nationality. I wouldn't have registered for the laissez-passer except that my wife panicked."

"A hundred thousand people panicked, not only me," his wife protested. "We would have been trapped."

"If only we had sold the house before the freeze," Mr. Sasson sighed. "But prices fell so low. And the ones who registered early had sold their assets without the government interfering. So I thought we could wait. How could I know the government would suddenly freeze the assets of all those who registered for the laissez-passer, and then confiscate them?"

"Easy dear, easy." Mrs. Dallal tried to soothe him. "Whatever you brought with you is good enough. Others lost everything in the banks and are living in tents now."

The conferences would last till dark, long after the Ashkenazim mothers—the European Jews—had called their children for supper. Slowly, reluctantly, the Iraqi immigrants would disperse, for, unlike Baghdad nights, those in Israel were damp and chilly. No more sleeping on the roof: gone were the long, breezy nights under the skies, with the cool bedding, the moon, the stars, and Allah above.

The chief instigator at these gatherings was Mr. Dallal, a frail man in his late sixties, with round, dancing eyes, a tiny moustache and a friendly, sociable disposition. He lived on the ground floor of the central building. Two or three times a week, Mr. Dallal would put on his tailored suit and take the bus to Tel Aviv. He would visit his money-lending brokers, fellow Iraqis like himself, collect his interest and bring back a full account to Mrs. Dallal. At home, he would sometimes shop for the groceries. But for the most part, his time was spent in the lobby. During the morning hours, he would sit outside on a stool, his fingers playing with amber beads, and try to engage the immigrant passersby in conversation; he would watch the small children play in the courtyard sand with their toy shovels, the older ones on their way to school---those Ashkenazi girls with their rosy cheeks, blue eyes and blond hair, were like heavenly creatures, but were they real Jews like him? And how about their snooty elders? There was the strong urge to confront them, to explain, to let out the anguish. Mr. Dallal would also watch the construction workers and strike up friendly conversations with them. But he made sure never to be conspicuous when Mr. Kamara's brother was among them.

"I don't want to embarrass him," he told his wife.

"Yes," she said. "It breaks my heart to see him carry the bags of sand and bricks. At his age! What happened to his money?"

"The freeze! Unfortunately, all his money was in the bank and the government took everything."

Mrs. Dallal, a jovial sixty-year-old woman with full cheeks and grayish hair, shared her husband's fascination for the lobby. Whenever she managed to get away from her housework—the new housework with no maid and no laundress—she would bring out a folding chair and join her husband.

"To get a feeling of space," she would explain to her fellow Iraqis and they would smile in sympathy.

"It is true," she would go on, breathing in the outside air. "I can't walk in the apartment. I keep knocking myself against the walls; it is as small as the servants' rooms back home."

"A wise person knows how to adapt to new situations," Mr. Zilka said.

"To adapt, to adapt," sighed Mr. Kamara.

"Mr. Kamara, the bricks are not comfortable," Mrs. Dallal said. "Let me get you a chair."

"No chair for me. The bricks are more suitable."

But Mrs. Dallal stood up, went into her apartment and came back with a folding chair. "Here."

"No, thank you." Mr. Kamara would not budge.

"Come on."

"I don't need a chair. Even the bricks are too good for me." Of all the grumbling immigrants on the premises, Mr. Kamara was the most vehement. He was a handsome, sixty-year-old man, dark-skinned and green-eyed. Unlike Mr. Sasson, he was not subject to outbursts of anger or lengthy speeches of outrage. He was the quiet, melancholy grumbler. A constant lobby companion to Mr. Dallal, he would come down from his third-story apartment, pick up a brick, station it against the wall, and sit with his arms folded around his knees. Mr. Kamara was not talkative. Most of the time, he would sit still and stare at the playground. He seldom participated in the immigrants' discussions except to emit one sigh after another.

"Mr. Kamara," Mr. Zilka suggested, "why don't you join the Ulpan—Hebrew teaching institute? Really. You would learn the language and then you could apply for a job."

"A desk job for an Iraqi?" Mr. Kamara sighed. "You must be joking. It's for the Ashkenazim only."

"But what do you propose to do?" Mr. Zilka went on.

"I'm leaving for Teheran as soon as I get a visa from my brother-in-law."

"Another Moslem country! Another Diaspora? Haven't you had enough?"

"No, I haven't."

"They all hate Jews. Do you believe they will let you . . . ?"

"If they won't, I know what I'll do. I will go up the Minaret and cry Allahwakbar—God is great."

"Mr. Kamara!"

"Is this any better?" Mr. Kamara snapped. "Look at my brother! At sixty, with a weak heart, he carries bags of bricks on his back. My poor mother must be turning over in her grave."

"He is so unhappy, his spirits are so low, I am afraid for his reason," Mrs. Kamara had talked about her husband to the other Iraqi women. "He insists on leaving for Teheran and the boys say they'll come back when they're of age. You know how the young love Israel, the freedom and all that. What kind of family would we be? The boys here and we there."

Another immigrant who seemed most affected by adjustment difficulties was Mrs. Sasson, a frail woman in her late forties, with curly brown hair and small features. She would sit in on the immigrants' conferences but would hardly voice an opinion or even take part in the conversation. "She's lost weight and doesn't sleep well at night," her husband said.

In addition to the grumbling and regret for the past, the sessions provided a vital exchange of information about the price of commodities, the distribution of rations, the location of the black market sources, the job and business fields; they also served to satisfy the desperate need to understand the new country and its values, to find one's way and place in it; to shed light on the enigmatic Ashkenazim, those creatures who, at first, were regarded with love, pride and admiration, then with curiosity, then mistrust, then. . . .

"They work as hard as bees," the immigrant mass study reported.

"Whenever they see my wife in the reclining chair on the terrace, they come to ask if she is ill or something," Mr. Sasson said.

"This is the Western world," said Mr. Zilka. "You strive, you compete, then you succeed."

"You want to succeed in order to relax later on. So why not relax from the beginning?" Mrs. Dallal said. "What kind of success is it when you can't take your time over a cup of coffee or a good conversation? Look at the Ashkenazim. Even when they talk, they're on the go. Look at their varicose veins!"

"They don't mind the hard work; they're used to it," Mr. Sasson said. "They didn't have it that rosy in Europe."

"Vote for the A party," the unrelenting loudspeaker roared into the evening, the breeze carrying the message far into the streets, the single-family homes and the apartment houses. "A is your party, the party of the union, the worker, the melting pot." Election. Another strange aspect of the new country. "Why should we melt in their pot and not they in ours?" Mrs. Dallal said. "After all, the Sephardim—the non-European Jews—are the majority."

At the beginning of June, as the weather grew warmer and the days longer, the sessions flourished into social gatherings. Toward dusk, the young people would return from work, the Ulpan or the army camp, join their elders and contribute their own observations to the general conclusions: the Ashkenazim know how to push their way. They are shrewd, shameless and so assertive! Real braggarts, no modesty at all.

These reports were confirmed by the children at school. With their restrictive, conservative upbringing, they were no match for the overconfident Ashkenazi children.

"And there is such solidarity among them. They would never allow a Sephardi any good position, not if they can help it."

"They built the country," Mr. Zilka said.

"So what?" cried Mrs. Dallal. "Don't we send our boys to the army?"

"Tell me the truth," persisted Mr. Zilka. "If you were the head of a company and you had to hire someone, wouldn't you prefer an Iraqi to an Ashkenazi?"

"No, I wouldn't," cried Mrs. Dallal. "Really, Mr. Zilka, you are 'plus royaliste que le roi.' To think that Jews who had suffered so much discrimination should now practice it, themselves, and what is more, on their fellow Jews! Just tell me, what's the difference? In Baghdad they called us Jews and here they call us Arabs."

"I can't stand Mr. Zilka." Mrs. Dallal went on raging long after Mr. Zilka had left. "I know his type. Inferiority complex about anything Iraqi and a blind admiration for anything Ashkenazi. They would like to copy the Ashkenazim in anything; bad or good, it doesn't matter."

"Instead of lamenting the past," Mr. Zilka offered his unasked-for advice to his fellow Iraqis, "better join an Ulpan, learn the language and then find a job. Look at the Iraqi men my age. They have their regular corner in King David's Park, a line of benches facing Bialik Street, and all they ever talk about is what this Bey had said and what this Pasha had done. They actually live in the past. Look at the Ashkenazim. . . ."

"Look at the Ashkenazim" had become a constant refrain, and the immigrants were taking a long, hard look. The Ashkenazim were everywhere; in the streets, the stores and offices, on the beaches, in the fields and hills. The three buildings were full of them, and they constantly hurried in and out of their apartments, brushing past the immigrants' gathering. The immigrants watched from a short distance. Both camps watched at some short distance—the immigrant men in tailored suits, the women in silk dresses; the Ashkenazim, men and women, in khaki shorts or pants, light blouses and biblical sandals. On the whole, the Ashkenazim were civil; whether condescending or purely friendly, theirs was a direct, explicit *Shalom.* Yet some of them were openly resentful:

"Where were you when the State was being built? You come now to sow the harvest, eh?"

Others were envious: "Do you call yourselves new immigrants? We are ten years in this country. We have been working like dogs and we don't have a refrigerator yet. And you come right away with everything."

"As though we have stolen the money from them," the immigrants answered, most of the time among themselves. "So some of us were lucky to smuggle some money, some valuables. . . ."

There were the arrogant and the bossy ones: "We will allow nothing short of European standards." Or the contemptuous: "You behave like Arabs. What is this pajama-wearing on the terraces? Pajamas are for bed only." And the immigrants would answer, again most of the time among themselves, that pajamas cover much more than those khaki shorts.

But there were the good-natured ones, friendly and curious: "Did you have a harem in Baghdad? Did you have cars or did you ride camels?" At which questions the immigrants would gasp in outrage.

And there were the responsible ones, concerned for the welfare of Israel and eager for the Iraqi immigrants to become dedicated, productive citizens: "You should work, work and study . . . The country is a melting pot . . . We will become one nation, all alike and equal. But you must work hard. And be patient. Be patient, it will be good. And you shouldn't have so many children. It's irresponsible."

The immigrant children with their smooth olive skin, large black eyes and exotic fiery look, were objects of concern, even love, by the Ashkenazim. "So cute, so sweet," they would say. They were the children of Israel, the future generation. That these children were undisciplined was no surprise, considering their background. The main complaint was that they would not stay home during the hours of rest. Two to four in the afternoon had been set aside by the Ashkenazim as the hours of rest, a necessary measure against the heat, the heat that was so disruptively non-European.

But the children would not abide by the rules. They would sneak out into the lobby, hide behind the columns and keep their activities at a low pitch until they lost all self-control and their shrill voices rang out in the corridor. Loud abuse would rain down from the terraces of the Ashkenazi households containing strong hints of the parents' culpability. Sometimes, if the transgressions were repeated, clear cold water would be poured on the children's heads, to the dismay of their mothers: "Those Ashkenazim. They don't care. They don't care if the children catch cold or get sick. And with this terrible humidity. And how can you imprison six children in boxlike apartments for two hours?"

It happened during one afternoon session while a hot discussion was going on. Mrs. Sasson was sitting among her fellow Iraqis when suddenly she stood up. "I must see about Eli. He runs around all the time." She sighed and walked off, her lean figure swaying on her high heels.

"It's the way with all children," called Mrs. Dallal. "He's your youngest. That's why you're after him all the time."

"He sweats a lot, then he starts coughing," Mrs. Sasson called back, and advanced to the edge of the community courtyard. She stood there, looking at the two-sided buildings and the playground. The square sandy lot had four wooden benches, two to each side. Children built and rebuilt sand designs with their toy pails and shovels. Seeing no sign of Eli, Mrs. Sasson turned back, her brown silk dress fluttering in the breeze. At the side entrance, she was accosted by Mrs. Einstein, an Ashkenazi neighbor in the building. Any encounter with the other camp was intriguing and, seeing the two women talking to each other, the immigrants stopped their conversation and sat back watching.

Mrs. Einstein was a forty-five-year-old buxom woman. Her fat thighs were clad in tight khaki shorts, the white compact flesh sensuously tickled by a few thin red veins. She spoke without interruption, gesturing and pointing at the courtyard. Mrs. Sasson blushed, crimsoned, then her eyes reddened. Her lips moved soundlessly, but she suddenly burst into tears and ran for the stairs.

"What is this?" cried Mr. Sasson, as he rushed to the Einstein woman, his fellow immigrants following. The Einstein woman looked stunned. She came forward, bringing her bewilderment to Mr. Sasson.

"I didn't tell her anything," she said. "I don't know what's the matter. I couldn't understand what she said. I didn't tell her anything."

"You didn't tell her anything!" Mr. Sasson moved his chubby form toward the woman and his hot breath blew over her tight shirt. "For nothing she is crying? For nothing? You listen to me. . . ."

"Wait, now wait," interceded Mr. Zilka. "What happened? What exactly did you tell her, Mrs. Einstein?"

"I just told her we could take pails of water and wash the lobby, she this side, me the other. That's all. Believe me."

"You tell my wife to wash the lobby?" Mr. Sasson howled. "You! She had two servants at home. You. . . ."

"I thought until we get somebody to do it."

"She'll wash the streets for you, my wife . . . ?"

"I'm sorry. I didn't think. . . ."

"You didn't think! You never think, you and your lobby, and your tiny worn carpet which you beat every day, raising the noise of hell. And what a carpet! A doormat, by God!"

"What has that got to do with my carpet? So I don't have an expensive Persian carpet," Mrs. Einstein's manner changed from bewilderment to haughty contempt. "I am sorry, I don't seem to understand you." She shrugged her shoulders and turned to leave. "Yes, you do," Mr. Sasson called after her. She stopped and turned to face him. "And you wouldn't hear my beating the carpet if you went to work instead of idling all day long." She rushed for the stairs.

"The, the . . ." Mr. Sasson stood at a loss, his face red to the ears.

"Take it easy," Mr. Zilka said. "Come now, let's go back."

Slowly, they returned to their corner and quietly sat down, some on the chairs, others on the bricks. They remained silent, looking at the small patch of sky visible above the three buildings.

"The bitch," Mr. Sasson grumbled to himself, and lifted his eyes toward the women. "Please excuse my language."

"It's all right," Mrs. Dallal chuckled. "Don't pay any attention to her. Arrogance! That's their specialty."

"True, true."

"Ha! Ha!" Mrs. Dallal began to laugh. "That part about the carpet is really funny. Can you imagine Mr. Sasson with his beautiful antique carpets, listening to the beating of doormats all day long?"

But Mr. Sasson would not cheer up. "Believe me they are better than us," he said sadly. "Look at that Einstein bitch. Each thigh worth one of our women. Strong and healthy. And look at my Sarina, so thin, the wind could blow her off. She lost ten kilos since we came here. And I do everything. I get up in the morning, prepare breakfast. . . ."

"She'll get used to it. Patience," Mr. Zilka said.

"And we have to start some business soon," Mr. Sasson went on. "What good is high interest when inflation is so high? Our money is dwindling. Soon it will be worthless. We have to start a business. Are we better than the Kadouris? They opened a grocery store. But go and tell Sarina. All she knows is how to cry. The other day she had to shame me in front of everyone. We were in Tel Aviv, when a procession of policemen passed by. 'Jewish policemen,' she said and the tears ran down. Such torrents! I don't know where she had them stored. Everyone turned to me: 'What's the matter with her?' Some gave me such looks, as though I had beaten her. I begged her to walk away, but, no, she had to see the whole precession, to the last one of them. What could you say to that? Believe me, they're better than we are. Each thigh is a woman."

"You're in love with their thighs, Mr. Sasson," Mrs. Dallal chuckled.

"He's right," Mr. Dallal conceded. "They are better than we are, much better suited for this hard competitive life. And we see it already, they're going up and we're going down."

". . . of the melting pot," the loudspeaker cut through the evening breeze. "Vote for A. A is your party. The party of the union, the party of the workers, the party of the melting pot."

Danse Macabre

Such a dismal day! Wait till Ezra wakes up and starts mumbling and whimpering: "Rain at this time of year! Rain when only last night the radio predicted a fine day. Rain. . . ." And his tongue would not stick to his mouth for the whole day. Well, what can you do? Some people are born grumblers. May God keep them healthy and grumbling. As my father, bless his memory, used to say: "He is a fool who tries to reform others."

Let's draw the curtains. Oh, it's pouring. Bless Ezra, his mouth will soon pour as much: "How could we have bought an apartment like this, a damp ground floor on the windy side, and the sun shut off by the next building? If you hadn't nagged and insisted on the Center, the Center, the Center!" He would go on accusing me and his head would swing like a seesaw.

What about him? Didn't he insist on a one-bedroom apartment instead of a studio? But with seven thousand liras, what could you buy except a ground floor? Seven thousand. The way the Israeli lira was melting we had to grab whatever came by. To think that we had exchanged a whole Iraqi dinar for a lira! The Center. The only thing I ever insisted upon in my whole life. No children, no grandchildren, if we don't need the Center, who does? On a main street with a line of benches where you can sit and watch passersby from everywhere. A hundred yards and you are in the park, and so close to the old folk's center. Not that Ezra uses it. And what family do we have, with me an only child? "An only child is like a single rose in a vase," Father, bless his soul, used to console Mother. "Standing alone, a rose has more beauty." But I could certainly use some brothers and sisters. Some people, may they enjoy it in good health, have such big families. Relatives everywhere, from east to west and north to south. If they were to visit every day, from sunrise till sunset, they wouldn't finish in months.

The only family we have is Ezra's brother, and Ezra had to dig up a quarrel with them. It is a small mind that holds on to grudges. As Father, may he rest in peace, used to say: "Even the entrails in the abdomen would quarrel."

I better hurry for the milk and bagels. So chilly, I would have liked to stay in bed. Why don't I let Ezra himself, go, since he keeps saying "I, myself, can go, I can go. . . ." But the time it takes him to dress and the fuss he makes. He screws a hole in your head: "Whom would I go to, Mirza or Lavine? Write down everything so that we don't go shopping all the time. Where's the umbrella, and why not keep it in the same place?" What has come over me today? I can't let go of the poor man. After all, it is his temperament. He can't help it. What makes me so edgy? Is it that trip to Jerusalem? Let me close the door quietly, as I go out. I don't want to wake him up.

It's not so bad outside. Only drizzling. Chilly, but so fresh and clean. The house is like a real box. People are already in the street. There goes that cute Braverman boy.

"*Shalom* cutie. How come so early? Kindergarten already?"

"No. I am going for the bagels." Such a sweetie with those big eyes and the small upturned nose. And the whipped-cream cheeks.

"You don't get them crispy if you come late," he said.

"Cutie wants them crispy, ha? Know what, I'll let you choose before me. You get all the crispy ones."

Isn't that Leah over there? She doesn't see me or she pretends not to. Maybe she's just too busy with her newspaper. I will greet her anyway. "*Shalom* Leah. I haven't seen you for some time. How are you, dear?"

"Fine, thank you." Such stiff greeting! Not even a smile. Some people think they're doing you a favor just by greeting you. As the wild wind blows, some fortunes are made and some fortunes are lost. She didn't have it that good, back in Baghdad. Now her nose is in the skies.

"And how are the children? God bless them."

"Fine, thank you. And you and Ezra?"

"Can't complain, thank God."

"Are you joining the Center's trip to Jerusalem?"

"No. Ezra won't go, and how can I leave him alone? The fresh air would be good for his health, but he won't listen."

"Did you call on Rosa?"

"No, dear. We didn't."

"You should go and break the ice."

"I know, dear, but what can I do? It's not up to me. I never was on bad terms with anyone, not in my whole life. You know me."

"Let me tell you, between us. She won't invite you to the wedding unless you call on her."

"No . . . I can't believe . . ."

"Oh, yes. I'm her cousin. I should know what I'm talking about. She says you didn't call to congratulate her, so she won't invite you. She says she won't have Ezra pick on each of her words, twist it and turn it upside down."

"What . . . well, dear, what can I do? Ezra is so stubborn."

"He's wrong."

"You tell him that."

"And why can't you tell him yourself? You're a wife of forty-five years, not a new bride. You've shared salt and bread with him for a whole lifetime. And don't give me that about his nervousness and his asthma. If he blows up, it wouldn't be your fault. A strong vinegar would blow up its own jar. Nobody could have been more patient than you."

"But Ezra is so . . ."

"Ezra with the frown engraved on his face, as though God owes him money. He can't rule your whole life. It's time he sees reason."

"You know how I love Rosa and the boys. . . ."

"You'll be the only one to lose. You need her. She doesn't need you. If you don't call to congratulate her, she won't invite you to the wedding. She'll let Ezra fry in his own rage."

"You're right. We should call on her but . . ."

"And believe me it's for your sake that I'm telling you all this. I wouldn't bother if it was for Ezra only. And maybe Rosa won't make any more wisecracks, if she ever did. She herself told me that all is vanity and what is the purpose of aggravating anyone?"

Oh God! That breathlessness in my chest. I can't even hear what Leah is saying. To think that Rosa would not invite us to the wedding! To think that she would dare! To tell the truth, what has poor Ezra done? He didn't answer her wisecracks or comment on them. He swallowed everything in silence. It's just that he didn't visit her or congratulate her; that's all. Would she dare not invite the boys' only uncle? So strong-willed, a real match for Ezra. And the way she quotes King Solomon, bless his memory, with her vanity adage, as though she is the fount of wisdom. Right after she harasses Ezra with one sting after another, getting bolder by the minute, she goes back to her "vanity, all is vanity." I'd better hurry. It may start pouring again.

That keyhole has to be oiled. The key doesn't go in smoothly. Ezra will complain that I woke him up. There, he's already awake, crouched up on the sofa and still in his pajamas. Is he small and thin? A bundle of strong, sore bones. What is the matter with me, my God? I should leave the poor man alone. I'm rather small myself, but certainly not so skinny.

"You're awake, Ezra."

"You woke me up when you closed the door, and I didn't sleep last night. You kept snoring all the time."

Look who is talking! His night siren could be heard for kilometers. There are times when I wake up thinking it's the telephone or the doorbell, and I never so much as brought it up to him. "Turn yourself into a grain," as my mother used to say, "and the chicks will eat you." But let it go. Soon I'll have to speak with him about Rosa. It is good that I met Leah today. Very sweet of her to advise me. And she was so insistent. Does Rosa want us to call or would she rather have Ezra roast in his rage? Leah is right; we need Rosa; she doesn't need us. With her big family, her many relatives, her three devoted successful sons, and enough money to. . . . Her husband was a shrewd businessman, and David, her eldest son, knew how to manage the inheritance. He also knew how to exchange the money. Three liras to the dinar. Maybe he still has some foreign currency left over. Not like Ezra, who couldn't rest until he had exchanged everything. And he wouldn't look for a job: "What kind of a job would I get, at my age?" He would say. "I don't know the language and I don't have a profession." It's been five years already. Probably he should have gone back and forth to the government employment office anyway. Maybe if he had been working, he wouldn't have come down with asthma. So many Iraqis suddenly developed asthma. "Because of their ordeal," people say. It might be true.

"Still raining." There he goes about the rain.

"Well, what can we do about it?"

"Did I ask you to do anything about it, Sima? I'm just worried about my asthma."

"Don't think about it and you won't have it."

"Is that so? Is that all there is to it? Some people have no fear of God. They chop salted onion on a wounded heart. It's all in my head, nothing real, just . . ."

"Oh dear, take it easy, Ezra. I didn't mean it that way. But, as the saying goes, speak of the devil and you invite him over."

"It's so chilly here. The dampness is gnawing at my bones." There he goes again. Don't I have my rheumatism, but do I ever whimper about it?

"I'll light the gas heater for you, Ezra."

"Oh, no! Do you want the smell of gas to choke me?"

"Take it easy. Louise has the heater on all day long. I'll light it on the terrace and then bring it in. It only smells at the beginning."

"It always smells."

"Listen, Ezra, let me try it. If it bothers you I'll shut it off, all right?"

"All right."

"I'll fill it up. They say it doesn't smell when it's full. It's so drafty on the kitchen terrace. All the smell will be gone."

So chilly outside; the north side is always cold. I'll have to straighten up that terrace. So many things piled up there. But where else can I put them? Not much space in a one-bedroom apartment. I better put the kettle on the stove; then I'll open the subject with Ezra.

"Ezra, I really would like to speak with you."

"Uh! Not the trip again? You go alone, Sima, and may God go with you. You enjoy yourself. . . ."

"It 's not the trip. It's Rosa." As though there is any hope of my ever going on that trip.

"Rosa, again! Stop pestering me, will you? Stop playing around with my soul. You don't want me to have a fit, do you?"

"Calm down, please, calm down. I won't speak about anything." See how he goes, and they tell me to stand up to him. They complain about nervous husbands. They should come and see this one. "And stop foaming and bubbling. It's not good for your asthma."

"Much you care."

Those grumblers! Always on the offensive. Crying "ouch" long before your prick them. Crying "ouch" while they prick others. They don't leave you time to think about attacking them. And believe me they are better off this way. So quarrelsome and gloomy, all you want is to satisfy them. And they all tell me to stand up to him. How can I? But I really shouldn't be afraid. It won't be my fault if he blows up and . . . a strong vinegar blows its own jar. I never saw vinegar prepared at home. I wonder if the strong ones really break their jar. It must be true or people wouldn't say it.

"Do you know, Ezra, that you behave exactly like a spoiled little boy? 'You must humor me, I have asthma. You mustn't speak about this, I have asthma. You . . .'"

"Oh God, what sin have I committed? Sima. . . ."

"And you complain like an old woman."

"I'm old. Isn't seventy-five old enough for you? You're twelve years younger."

"I have twice as much white hair, and look at my teeth."

"Shall I dye my few black hairs white? Shall I extract my remaining teeth? Would that make you happy, Sima? Would it, would it?"

"Stop screeching, please, calm down, calm down. Come and have some tea. Come to the kitchen." I'd better lead him myself or he won't budge. So much nerve in such a small bundle of bones. No, not a bundle of bones. A bundle of explosives! Such strength in a seventy-five-year-old. What am I saying? May he keep strong and healthy and outlive me. What would I be doing alone? A childless woman with so little money. But the chores and expenses would be cut in half. Such dreadful thoughts. Oh, God, what's happening to me today? I'm sinning. The devil got in me. I must go to the synagogue for penitence this Friday. I must. How many years left for me anyway? Fifteen at most, maybe more. But they will be over before you know it. How strange that one has to go. You feel so well-rooted and then suddenly . . . Those black gloomy thoughts never pester you when you're outside, with people. That's why one should go out a lot. But go and tell Ezra. He never was much for going out. In Baghdad it was an uncle who had died and then there was a cousin—a good excuse for him to stay home. I kept telling him that once you reach fifty there's always someone going off, and if you plan to mourn each one of them, you may as well stay in your box forever. It's so different in Israel; nobody observes these things anymore. But we stay the same. We never go to a movie here. Even when Ezra finally agreed to see *Exodus*, he chose to be sick that week. And when I dared to ask him to go to a coffee shop, he said, "My father never went to one."

"See, Ezra. The heater doesn't smell. I'll put an orange peel near the flame to kill the smell of gas. So warm and cozy in the kitchen and these bagels taste so good. Take some more cheese, Ezra." Nothing like drinking tea with someone; drinking it alone has no meaning. As Ezra says, tea is compassionate, soothing. I hope it soothes him really well. Do I have the nerve to try again?

"You feel warm and good with the tea, ha Ezra? Is it worth it to get so worked up over nothing? Believe me, if it wasn't for what I heard today, I wouldn't bother you."

He swallowed his tea in silence. He didn't blow up. He wants to know what I heard today. Let him finish his breakfast and I'll start again. I have to. "Would you like some more tea, Ezra? No? Then I'll put the heater in the hall. There, sit near it. Put your feet on top. I really have to speak with you."

"How many times do we have to discuss Rosa? Go ahead, Sima. Better get it over with." That miserable whining tone.

"Let me talk just for a little while. Will you promise to stay cool? That's the main thing."

"Go on, go on."

"Well, first, let me tell you one thing. Rosa is your brother's wife, not my brother's. This is your family, so you can't say I am siding with them. Second, we don't have many close relatives. I'm an only child and we are childless. A piece of good luck I met with."

"Will you stop hinting it was my fault?"

"When did I ever say that?"

"Your family blackened my name often enough. To go to a doctor and shame myself in front of everyone. In Baghdad, who goes to a doctor for something like that? Anyway, why didn't you leave me?"

"Shall I go on with what I was going to say?"

"Yes, go on, go on."

"You made me forget. Well, what I mean is that someone in our position shouldn't dwell on every little word and . . ."

"Every little word! How can you say that, Sima? Each time we visit her she makes my dead dance before my own eyes! My poor father and mother. And Heskel, my brother. Each time we go there she dips me in the salt of her tongue then fries and grills me with her venom. And don't tell me it was the last time only. Remember when you told her she was efficient and she said, 'Once a viper tongue said that I have length but not depth.' Don't you think I knew she meant my mother?"

"Maybe not. How do you know? I don't remember words. You know me. And I don't hold grudges. If I were to remember all the harsh words that have been said to me. . . ."

"There goes Saint Marie."

"Yes, really. Father, bless his memory, used to say that life is too short to be wasted on squabbles. And you shouldn't hold on to every little word. . . ."

"Every little word! Leave me alone, Sima. I don't know what has come over you today, but please leave me alone. I've swallowed from this woman until I said enough. Last time she went too far."

"She won't invite us to the wedding unless we call on her."

"How do you know?"

"I met her cousin Leah this morning."

"I can't believe it." He is turning yellow and green. "I'm the uncle of the bridegroom. I never quarreled or said any harsh word to her or the boys. We just didn't call on her for one month, two at most."

"But we didn't congratulate her on the engagement and it's her eldest son. She told Leah that you pick up her words, spin them, wind them. . . ."

"But the boys. . . . I'm their uncle, in place of their father."

"They won't upset her because of you. They're devoted to her and you're putting them in a spot. And remember the famous proverb 'Kiss the hand that you cannot bite.'"

"What kind of men are they? Don't they have a mind of their own? I'm their uncle."

"She's their mother. Remember how devoted you were to your mother?"

"Well." He is really shaking now. "If they won't invite me, then they won't invite, so I won't go to the wedding."

"It is not the wedding that bothers me, Ezra. It's the break. The break that would come between you and them. They're your nephews, the sons of your older brother and, God blesses them, all of them are doing so well."

"I'm not going to ask them for money. The little that we have. . . ."

"I know. But remember how pleasant they were when you were at the hospital. They visited so often and helped with all the arrangements. They spoke with the doctors and nurses and told them to take good care of you."

"I don't need anyone to speak with the doctors or nurses. This is Israel; thank God, the doctors are Jewish and the nurses are Jewish."

"But it's a different feeling when you have people caring about you. She didn't mean it about your parents, Ezra."

"No, didn't she? Everything sets her to comparing here with Baghdad. It's been such a long time, but she never forgets. What does she want? To get even, to take it on me, now? What a black heart that woman has. 'What did we get for fathers-in-law and mothers-in-law in Baghdad? Whores and pimps.' My God, she makes my dead dance before my very eyes. No, no, she just went too far."

"'In-laws in Baghdad were like whores and pimps,' she said. She was speaking in general, not about your parents. Anyway Leah said she won't talk like that any more." Wouldn't she really? I want to calm him down but I don't believe she will stop. She enjoys it too much. But then who knows? "Besides, don't listen to her, Ezra. Think of the boys, their father is dead, you stand in his place. Don't put them on a spot. Be the wise one and give in. As the saying goes, a thousand friends and not one enemy."

"My poor brother. She must have killed him."

"Come now, no woman could have killed a brother of yours."

"True, he was a real man. She couldn't open her mouth then."

"But we need them . . . Such fine boys and so respectful . . . They were so helpful when you were at the hospital with your asthma . . . We are practically alone . . . They are our only close relatives . . . Kiss the hand that you cannot bite . . . Think of your brother. . . ."

I couldn't sleep last night. I kept tossing and turning in bed, thinking about a dress for the wedding, a suit for Ezra, the present. . . . Sometimes I feel like staying in bed, covering myself with a blanket and sleeping everything off. And I couldn't tell Ezra about it. "We didn't go yet," he would have complained, "and you already. . . ." I'd better get up. Such a nice day. It's good to know you have somewhere to go, and Rosa serves such goodies. We'll visit in the afternoon. So, according to Leah, Rosa won't annoy Ezra anymore. Good for him. He made a fuss, scared her and got his way. It pays to be strong. As my mother used to say, "Even God is afraid of the strong." Not that He, glorified be His Name, is afraid of anyone. But everybody loves peace and God is no exception. What can you do? Not everyone is a strong vinegar. Look at me. Didn't I get enough from my in-laws in that big old house with Ezra's mother and father presiding over everyone's acts and words? Did they ever tire of hinting at my being childless, 'a useless barren tree,' and their sons repeating the hints like parrots? But Rosa was always kind. She never feared my evil eye on her children. She let me hold them as much as I wanted and insisted they show me all respect. How could my in-laws imply that I am barren when it was most likely their son's fault? Otherwise why did he refuse to see a doctor, and when he finally did, he chose to go alone and came back saying the doctor found nothing wrong with him? "It's what killed your father," Mother used to say. Poor Father, he never mentioned it, except for once, "If he had known that he was sterile, he shouldn't have married, certainly not an only child." Poor Father, he died an angel's death. Reading in his chair, he passed away in two minutes. I wish I could die that way. Mother soon followed. "You should divorce him," she used to say in the last days of her illness. As if it was that easy. Who divorced in those days? And after a while it really didn't matter. When you want something so badly and for so long, and then you don't get it, you end up not caring. In the end it doesn't matter what you get and don't get in life. What matters then? But really, do I want now to take care of a bunch of children, to worry about their doing this or that? What are children, anyway? You waste your whole life caring and catering and get very little in return. It's just that when you get old you want someone to look after you, to be there when something happens, to recite the Kaddish after you: "God full of mercy. . . ." Ezra is better off than I am. At least he has someone twelve years younger, someone to take care of him, to mourn him. But you never know. I may go first.

88

Danse Macabre

"I'll prepare the white linen shirt for you, Ezra."
"I don't want it. It makes me look dead pale."
"But it's so elegant and the couple might be there. You must wear it."

I'm glad it's a beautiful day. A sunny glow on God's world and its creatures.
"Sit on the bench, Ezra. Another bus will come very soon."
"They don't come that often in the afternoon."
"But it's good that there's a bench. Not all stations have benches."
It's rush hour and the bus will be jammed with people returning from work. I hope there will be a seat for Ezra. I love our location. Two minutes from the bus and everything is so near. All the nearby apartment buildings have stores on their ground floors. You can buy everything nearby. The groceries, the vegetables and fruit stores are right across the street. It's a wide and airy street with a narrow garden lane in the middle, stretching as far as the Lawless movie house. You don't have to go to the park; you just cross the street to the garden lane, sit on a bench under a eucalyptus tree and watch the young mothers with their children playing with the sand. Old people also come to sit on the benches. That Handler woman from across the street is very friendly. She likes to talk with me and Ezra. With our broken Hebrew we manage quite well.

To think that at the last minute Ezra shrank back and wanted to stay home. I had to coax him again and again. He wanted me to go by myself. But it's his family, and I am not used to going out alone. Besides, the change will do him good. Otherwise it's home, the bed, the park, home, the bed.

There is the bus. It doesn't look like there's an empty seat for Ezra. So many boys and it's past school time. Such a lovely boy, and the way he said, "Here sir, have a seat." You wouldn't think they know how to behave, not with the shouting and the laughing. What are they so excited and happy about? Every word that they utter calls for laughter. I'm smiling in spite of myself. God, they must think I'm crazy.

"Here we are. I'll go down first. Come now, let me hold your hand, Ezra."

"Those boys are so noisy and no one tells them to shut up."

"That's the way with young people, Ezra." He really has a salty tongue. Living with him for so many years, I hardly notice it now. It's only when someone points it out, like Leah today, that I really pay attention.

Just a few yards to Rosa's apartment. It's a healthy walk for Ezra. Hebat Zion Street is wide and bright. All the apartment houses are new, luxurious, and the entrances have marble floors. The villas and the two-family houses are elegant too. But it's a shame that Rosa chose an apartment on the third floor. Those stairs. With her kind of money she could have bought an apartment on a second floor. Anyway it's better than a damp ground floor.

"I don't feel like going in, Sima. Let's go back home."

"What? Do I have to talk about it with you all over again? She won't make any more wise remarks, believe me. And if she does, we'll leave. Come on, now. Take your time. Hold on to the rail and rest in between."

Why am I so nervous, myself? So what if she acts cold or makes faces? At least we have done our share.

There is Doron opening the door. "*Shalom* uncle, *Shalom* aunt. Come on in. I haven't seen you for some time. Sit outside on the terrace, please. I'll call Mother."

Bless him, his flowing talk and his giant steps. He looks so big. How old is he now? Twenty-two? Yes, he's the youngest. He takes after Rosa. Tall, dark and big-featured. But on a man, it's very becoming. He was welcoming, all right. What would a lively young boy care about squabbles between his old mother, his uncle, and dead grandparents?

That living room is really big. It's a beautiful three-bedroom apartment with a large kitchen and two terraces. Rosa bought the best furniture. The living room has a beautiful mahogany blue velvet set—a sofa and two chairs, and a four-door breakfront.

Rosa is taking her time, like a queen. I wonder when she will appear. Oh, there she is. Such a dark dress! It makes her look so grim, with those big black eyes, piles of grayish hair and the thick eyebrows. I don't like to comment, but with that olive greenish complexion, she really shouldn't wear dark clothes.

"Hello, dear Rosa, how are you? Congratulations, dear. I'm so happy."

"Thank you, Sima."

"Congratulations." That Ezra! A stiff congratulation is all he can manage.

"Thank you, Ezra. Why don't you sit between us in the armchair? It is more comfortable."

"Yes, move Ezra. Sit where Rosa tells you." She's being really considerate, letting bygones be bygones, offering him the big armchair. But there's something severe about her even when she tries to be nice. Not even a smile. As though she's ashamed of being too nice.

"We couldn't come earlier, dear. Ezra wasn't feeling well, you know."

"I understand. It's the time of the year. Now hot, now cold."

"I love your terrace, dear. It faces the street where you can see everyone."

"We also could have managed a terrace on the street, Sima." Ezra has to butt in. "But of course you had to have the Center." There he goes with his complaints about me.

"A woman needs the Center for shopping. It's quite a chore." Listen to her! Isn't that nice, the way she corks him off? She always does it when he starts complaining about me, with her shrug and that haughty jerk of the head. Her comments allow no arguments. They are final, period, as though it is beneath her to discuss them.

"There's a trip to Jerusalem from the old folk's center. Would you like to go, Rosa?"

"My dear Sima. You know me by now. I am not one to play young, going to lectures and trips. We've missed everything, the way we were brought up in Baghdad. What's left isn't worth much." The knowledgeable Rosa. With her three boys and many relatives she can well afford to stay home. Even her two terraces are enough. They adjoin the neighbors' terraces and she can chat as much as she wants.

"But I never do, believe me, Sima," she always says. Well, I was hoping she might go on the trip; then maybe I could have coaxed Ezra to join. But no. People like Ezra know how to bury themselves alive. The trouble is that they drag others with them.

She's going to the kitchen now. So convenient, this terrace, leading to the living room and the kitchen as well. The kitchen is as large as a room, with wood cabinets all around. Here come the almonds, the fruits and sherbet, and those delicious Turkish sweets.

"Please sit down, Rosa. We didn't come to tire you, dear. Did the engaged couple buy an apartment, in good health?" I have to start a conversation or else we'll all fall asleep.

"Yes, Rehovot. That is where her parents live."

"But that's so far from you."

"My dear Sima, now-a-days. . . ." She looked at Ezra and stopped. She's afraid to annoy him. Isn't that pleasant? He made a fuss and got her scared. Good for him, really.

"At least they could have chosen somewhere in between."

"I'm not going to compete with anyone over anything, Sima." Rosa and her detached wisdom, her "Solomon's vanity" adage. She suddenly dismisses the whole world as though it were beneath her slipper. But I know a different Rosa. I know how her big eyes blaze, how her mouth quivers, and her words, salted and peppered, come out like stings and pricks.

"Even so, you need your son near you. David is your eldest and you're close to him. After all you nursed and raised. . . ."

"Really, Sima, do you think I would visit them that often? Let them come when they will."

"Did you hear about the price-rise in bread?" Ezra with his remarks from nowhere. What has bread got to do with the subject?

"No. When was that?" Rosa seems interested.

"Shall we meet the couple today, Rosa? I would love to see the bride." People say she is pretty.

"I don't think they'll come, Sima. They have so much shopping to do and they haven't ordered the furniture yet."

"Don't you go shopping with them?"

"Who, me? You must be joking, Sima." Again she looks at Ezra. She can't be that scared of him?

"The price of rice will go up too." There goes Ezra with his gloomy news broadcasts.

The kettle is summoning Rosa to the kitchen. She walks very straight for her age. How old is she, seventy? Ezra claims she's his age. But it doesn't seem likely. She looks much younger. Ezra is squinting at me. What does he want?

"Sima, listen, don't . . ."

"Hush, aren't you glad we came? Did you see how she seated you in the armchair?"

"Sima, will you please . . ."

"She's coming."

Here she is, carrying the beautiful china set on a tray. The delicate smell of the tea with the cardamom. The whole terrace is steaming with the aroma. Ezra is holding out his hand for the china cup, like a beggar. He always says that tea is soothing, merciful.

"Did you buy a dress for the wedding, in good health?"

"Not yet, Sima. It isn't that easy."

"You should ask the bride to go with you."

"My dear Sima, this is not Baghdad where young people were their elders' slaves. This is Israel, the other extreme. And we got both bad ends of the deal. Both bad ends of the deal. Now . . ."

What a splash! "What's the matter, Ezra? Oh my God, what happened?" I'm trembling.

"Nothing, Sima. He must have been crunching an almond while he drank the tea. Here, take a napkin, Ezra. It's nothing."

Such coolness and such blazing eyes. She's right. It's nothing. But, look at his face. He's struggling for breath.

"Oh, my God, what shall I do, Rosa?"

"Don't panic, Sima. And you, Ezra, stand up, up." She's so strong; she pulls him with one arm. "Sima, hold him by the other arm. Yes, hold him by the other arm and let's each shake him from one side. Don't panic, just shake him with me. Cough it up, Ezra, come now." She's so big, and those flaming eyes and quivering mouth. God, we're

shaking him so hard, like we're shaking a tree. Seeing us, people
would think we're murdering him.

"Aren't we shaking him too hard, Rosa dear?"

"No, we are not."

But she has stopped shaking him. She pats him on the back, instead. She actually is hitting him on the back. So hard! Look at her
chattering teeth.

"Now, hit him on the back, Sima, from your side. I'm taking care
of my side. Harder, harder, Sima. Cough it up, Ezra. Come on, don't
fight. Cough it up. Let go. Don't fight, I say. There, you see, you're
okay now! Sit back in the armchair."

Thank God. He's breathing again. He looks so white. "Yes, sit
down, Ezra. I don't know how to thank you, dear Rosa. I don't know
what I would have done without you. It's so hard for me to manage
him alone."

"Don't I know it?" She is smiling now, with that owlish twinkle in
her eye.

"He scares me and I panic so easily." See the way Ezra eyes me?
You would think he is seeing me for the first time.

"I can well imagine. And listen, Ezra. The trouble with you is that
you don't let go. You fight too much."

"I was afraid I would be strangled."

"Nonsense. It's just a cough." She is laughing now.

"I really don't feel well, Sima. We'd better go home." He's always
in a hurry to go home and now he has his pretext.

"But why?" Rosa asks. She doesn't want us to leave, bless her.
"You're all right now. It was just a cough. Come on, stay a while."

He's standing like a rock and if we don't go now, he'll blame me for
it and complain about it for days.

"I think he wants to go, dear Rosa. Another time."

"Oh, all right. But come again."

"You know how I love to come here, Rosa." It's true. I'm not flattering her. "The way you handled Ezra today, you have a way with
everything. And I always love to be with you."

"I feel the same way about you, Sima. Seeing you, I see my own past before me. We have so much in common. So make it often. I don't like to travel and the boys are busy with their own life. So make it every week. Is Wednesday all right with you?"

"Oh, fine. I'll bring him every Wednesday." Wednesday is good. Tuesday I do the laundry and on Wednesday I do the ironing.

"Wait, Sima. Let me bring you the invitation."

"Don't bother now, dear. We'll get them next Wednesday. Goodbye, dear Rosa. God bless you and thank you again."

"Goodbye."

"Be careful, Ezra." I don't want him to fall and blame me later. "Let me hold your hand. Wednesday is a good day. Tuesday I do the laundry and Wednesday the ironing. Your white linen shirt will be ready."

She Couldn't Say No

The head of the Iraqi Jewish Cultural Committee and the councilman of Kiryat Shlomo came to see her one sunny, breezy afternoon. The guard at the gate directed them to the third floor, toward the left end of the corridor, internal medicine room 203.

She shared room 203 with two other patients. Her bed, against the window, was slightly tilted and she sank under the sheets, her white head barely touching the pillow. She saw them approaching and smiled while her hand went to smooth her wild thin hair. The councilman spoke about honoring roots, pride in historical background and folkloric tradition, but she could not grasp what he actually wanted. Her blank look spoke for itself.

"We are celebrating the 25th anniversary of the Iraqi immigration to Israel." The councilman became more specific. "We will remember the old life, revive the Iraqi Jewish tradition of the past, yours and mine. We'll sing all the old songs, the holiday songs, the wedding songs, the Bar Mitzvah's, the Brisses, and you will sing and play the tambourine."

"Me?" She choked, then smiled in disbelief. *"Bdalak."*—I give my life for you, an Arabic, fawning servile expression.

"Yes, you."

"In my condition, *Bdalak*? Look for another *Dkaka*—tambourine player."

"There are no others. They're all dead."

"You're the best," blurted the head of the cultural committee, dismayed at his colleague's insensitivity, categorizing the poor woman with the dead or the soon-to-die. "And you don't have to sing. We have other singers. Enough if you play the tambourine. We just want an authentic *Dkaka*."

"Can I really play the tambourine now, *Bdalak*?" Each one of her sentences ended with "*Bdalak*," the legacy of humility that had been her lot in Baghdad where the poor remained forever poor and she, entertaining at happy occasions, would wait for the meager tips that barely sustained her and her family. Could she not shake off that "*Bdalak*," now in Israel, with the equality of classes, opportunities for all, education for all, her children well off, her grandchildren at the university?

"Yes, you can play," the head of the cultural committee answered. "And all the important Iraqis will be there: the Minister of Agriculture, The Head . . . even The Chief of Staff."

"God bless him," she murmured.

"You wouldn't want to disappoint the Chief of Staff?"

"*Bdalak!*" She, disappoint the Chief of Staff! The Nobel hero, defender of the land, the hallowed David who had defeated Goliath. He was an Iraqi Jew, the son of the ancient, biblical Heskel. She remembered Baghdad's Moslems labeling all Jews "Heskel-beware-the-shell." "Heskel-beware-the-shell" was her husband, her son, her cousin . . . meek cowards, trembling at the sight of their shadow, harassed and persecuted. Let them beware this son of Heskel, the proud lion of Judea, lest his wrath pierce their shield. She knew him from television. Young, strong, handsome; he walked with a sure, firm step, his tall figure stooped . . . saddled by concern for his recruits. His sideburns prematurely gray, in sorrow for the fallen . . . young babes whose beards had not yet sprouted, and his sleepless vigilant eyes wandering toward the far-off fields, the treacherous fields. . . .

"It will be the day after tomorrow," the councilman said. "You will wear the long dress and the black scarf with that fringe of coins."

"I don't have it. I threw it away." Why would she keep it, the reminder of her miserable years, a widow in heartless Baghdad, knocking on doors, clowning for a living—what a stigma in those days! She would twist the words, rhyme the lines, pour deserved and undeserved praise, her tambourine evoking applause. In later years, when European music became the fashion and the rhumba and the zamba filled the air, she would be dismissed with a tip, like a beggar, her song spurned, her tambourine ignored.

"I will not give permission for her to leave the hospital." The doctor shook his head. "What is the matter with you? Don't you see how sick she is?"

"The event is important," the councilman began. "It strengthens one's pride in one's heritage, and when the general welfare is at stake, the individual discomfort. . . ."

"General welfare indeed! Is she saving the world for you? You just said she's going to play for fifteen minutes only, and you have a four-hour program, so skip her."

"But it's a shame because she is the only living *Dkaka*, the last one. Besides, she herself wants to come. She really does. Ask her."

"Well . . . let me talk to her."

The doctor joined the two men as they returned to Internal Medicine, room 203.

"What is this, Gveret Shamash?" the doctor asked. "These gentlemen tell me you want to play at their party. You know you're sick, don't you?"

"The Chief of Staff . . ." Her broken Hebrew was hardly intelligible.

"What . . . ?" The doctor looked puzzled, then he understood. He remained silent for a few seconds. "All right," he said finally, and turned to the two gentlemen. "But take very good care of her."

The head of the Jewish Iraqi Cultural Committee and the council-man of Kiryat Shlomo picked her up from the hospital and drove her to the town's large theater building. Two young women met her at the door and helped her backstage. They dressed her and pampered her. Then they took her onto the stage and sat her on that low, authentic stool. She held her tambourine and waited.

The curtain opened and rainbow lights blinded her as she tried to peer through the sea of heads and clapping hands. There was some announcement on the loudspeaker and more applause erupted. Then the music started and her old songs began to hammer in her ears. She battered the drum in a frantic race with her heartbeat, the rainbow lights and clapping hands swirling in her head.

Finally she was led backstage to lie down on a reclining chair amid hectic in—and—out traffic, with the old melodies beating through the walls. She watched, listened and listened, and then she saw him, the Chief of Staff in person heading backstage. All around him, people mumbled and gesticulated. He approached her, a halo on his forehead. He had come to meet her.

"You came straight from the hospital," he said.

"*Bdalak.*"

"Thank you so much." He bent down and kissed her hand.

Tears came into her eyes. She wanted to . . . but a thick haze enveloped her, dimmed her sight and paralyzed her tongue.

Back at the hospital, the haze grew thicker. For three days she alternated between pain, coma and hallucinations; she hallucinated about rainbow lights, the big, big party, the old, old songs, and on the fourth day she died, the Chief of Staff's kiss on her hand.

Retribution

We and the Kasmas were the only Iraqi Jewish families in the new four-story apartment building on Hibat-Zion, Ramat-Gan; the rest were Ashkenazim: European Jews. The building was ten yards wide, forty yards long. It consisted of two sections: The front and the back, each with a separate entrance. It had a broad brick-paved sidewalk, a narrow lane along each of its sides leading to a small backyard. The left lane ended with a strip of ground intended to be a flower bed.

The building was completed in February and the tenants began moving in. They dedicated the first week to exploring the new neighborhood: How far were the nearest grocery store, the kindergarten, the schools? How many buses nearby, their stations, their routes?

Within two weeks, the tenants knew almost everything about each other. Those I had encountered asked me about myself, told me about themselves, filled in the gap about the ones I hadn't met: their professions, the number of their children, their years in Israel. Soon I became friendly with a Mrs. Zukerman, a tenant of Polish origin who, like me, had been in Israel for only two years.

"How come the Zukerman woman is hanging around you?" Mrs. Kasma asked me. "Those Ashkenazim. They never befriend anyone without some ulterior motive."

"Exactly," Mrs. Kasma's husband said.

I would not accept the notion that Mrs. Zukerman befriended me for any reason except that I am interesting, intelligent. . . .

"To me it doesn't matter whether a person's color is white, black, brown or green," Mrs. Zukerman would say. The comment was for my benefit. There were no blacks or Asians in Israel then. There were only European Jews who were fair-skinned and Middle Eastern Jews, called Sephardim, who were olive-skinned or dark. Mrs. Zukerman was declaring that to her all Jews were the same. As to her high opinion of me, it was quite apparent whenever we argued. "How can you say that? You, such a wise, intelligent person," she once told me. And from then on I seldom disagreed with her.

The Kasmas were my adjacent neighbors. We had terraces facing the east, and each morning we enjoyed an hour-long streak of sun which sneaked into the space between our building and the next one. Mrs. Kasma and I made it a point to relish these short moments of sunshine.

"It's so chilly in the apartment," I once said.

"The same with us," Mrs. Kasma answered.

"We should have bought on a higher floor. We saw the apartment when the house was still a skeleton and there seemed to be plenty of sun then."

"The same with us," Mrs. Kasma said. "In this country you must have a hundred eyes, especially when there is no one to advise you. Our family and friends are also new in the country, so there was no one to help us."

"In two or three years, we might sell and buy a better apartment. I'm thinking of taking a job as soon as my son Ariel is five years old."

"That's a good idea," Mrs. Kasma said. "Many Ashkenazi women work even though they have children. That's the way to advance in this country."

The Kasmas had a son and two daughters. The son, nineteen years old, was serving in the army. The daughters, married and with children, lived nearby and the grandchildren, aged three to six, visited their grandparents quite often. When they arrived in Israel, the Kasmas had bought a two-bedroom apartment. But Mr. Kasma was unable to find a job, so they opted to sell, buy a one-bedroom apartment and use the difference in money to open a business. He decided on a vegetable store near his new apartment, so he could come home to eat and nap during the lunch break. Also it was easy for Mrs. Kasma to go back and forth and help him out. Unfortunately the venture proved to be a failure and, unable to make ends meet, Mr. Kasma finally had to sell the store.

"It is not his kind of work," Mrs. Kasma explained. "To get good merchandise, you have to be up at the market as early as four o'clock in the morning. Not only that, but you have to push and shove with hoodlums and fight with them over the good merchandise. How can he do that? He used to be a supervisor in. . . ."

Mr. Kasma finally found a job as a salesman in a grocery store and to make a few extra liras, he often brought home a few cartons of eggs and sold them to family and friends.

Mr. Kasma was a tall, handsome man of sixty. He walked straight and his white hair gave him an air of distinction. Yet he was shy, or rather he belonged to the old school of Iraqi men who deemed it unbecoming to be talkative with women lest their behavior might be interpreted, God forbid, as more than friendly. I met him quite often since his going to work coincided with my taking Ariel to kindergarten. His *Shalom* to me was always curt and hurried, yet there were times when he would overcome his shyness and stop to chat. I learned to recognize these occasions as connected to some personal trouble with one of "those Ashkenazim."

"Did you hear what this, may God erase his name, has done?" Mr. Kasma would confide in me. "If I had been an Ashkenazi, would he have dared?" These were the early fifties. The mass immigration of Jews from Arab lands had eased, the food rations and long bus queues

had stopped, but the Sephardim's resentment of perceived discrimination remained at its height.

One of Mr. Kasma's clashes had been with Mr. Austrovski, the
owner of the coffee shop in the building. The ground floor of the
front building consisted of two stores; the one to the right had not
been sold yet; the one to the left had been purchased by Mr. Austrovski who had turned it into a café. Both stores were five yards wide but
while the one on the right was six yards long, the café store extended
to the end of the back building. Mr. Austrovski used the front as a café
and ice cream parlor, one part of the following remaining space as a
restaurant, and the rest as his own one-bedroom apartment. Soon
Mr. Austrovski annexed the narrow lane courtyard along his premises, closed it off with a fence at the back end, and turned it into an
outdoor dining place for his restaurant customers.

All the tenants objected. It was clearly specified in everyone's
contract that the building had a courtyard all along its three sides,
in addition to the front sidewalk. A house meeting was called and
the unanimous decision demanded that Mr. Austrovski remove the
fence. Mr. Austrovski did not heed the tenants' decision, claiming a
verbal understanding with the builder which allowed him the use of
the courtyard. Eventually the tenants gave in. Some had no children
and didn't care about the size of the courtyard; others argued that the
matter required expensive litigation which would be useless, since
Mr. Austrovski would chase away the children anyway and they, in
turn, had better not play there for fear that they might hit the glass
doors and get hurt. One issue remained unsettled though; the kitch-
en terraces of the middle and back apartments were directly above
the café yard and the rows of laundry rods stretched up to the fourth
floor. There was no problem for those who sent their laundry out. But
Mrs. Kasma performed the task at home, and soon Mr. Austrovski directed his shouting at the dripping laundry. Mr. Kasma shouted back,
pointing at Mr. Austrovski's swindling his side of the backyard.

"Would any of us Iraqis dare push his way around like this?" Mr.
Kasma asked me the next day. "What's more, right after the argument, I met Mr. Austrovski on my way out and he greeted me as

though nothing had happened and we were the best of friends. Typically Ashkenazi."

Soon the store next to the café was bought by a real estate agent, Mr. Shamash, of Iraqi origin, who, twenty years before, had immigrated to Israel. He was a tall, heavily built, dark man, around fifty years old. His thick eyebrows and big features gave him a severe look, but the impression was soon dispelled by his suave, drawing-room manners. He was especially smooth in the presence of women. Seeing one, his face would light up, a sly smile would waver at the corner of his mouth and he would flip to attention and discreet courtship.

"I like him," said Mrs. Zukerman. "I like him very much. He makes you feel every inch a woman. Besides, he's quite intelligent. A man of the world, so unlike Mr. Kasma."

I agreed.

The tenants elected a three-member committee to take care of the building's affairs and Mrs. Zukerman was one of them. Her task was to collect maintenance money and keep the expense account. It seemed to suit her well. She was a fifty-year-old survivor of the Nazi camps, married to a supervisor in the government. They were childless. Mrs. Zukerman did not work and therefore had plenty of time on her hands. Sociable and friendly, she enjoyed calling on the tenants, collecting the maintenance fees and chatting. She seemed interested in everything and everyone. "I love people," she would tell me.

She was a small, blond woman, with a round face and light brown eyes. She had a milky complexion, slightly freckled and unusually wrinkled for her age. She attributed that to her behavior when she came out of the concentration camp. She ate non-stop, became fat, and when she finally lost weight, her face wrinkled and she developed heart trouble. She was still plump, but she took meticulous care of her appearance. She had her hair done every week, along with manicures and pedicures. She dressed in youngish clothes, wore high heels, walked straight and very slowly, because of the high heels or perhaps the heart trouble. She never seemed in a hurry.

"Why should I be?" she told me. "Who's running after me? I like everything and everybody. And I'll take my time." She explained that while for me breakfast might mean clearing the table and getting rid of the morning dishes, to her it meant deliciously aromatic coffee, crispy tantalizing rolls and soft, smooth butter. She took pleasure in going to the grocery store where the owner and his wife talked to her about their lives, hopes, disappointments. . . . She derived the same pleasure from the laundry man, the hairdresser, the milkman and even the bus driver. In Israel one can become friendly with everyone if one chooses and, often, if one doesn't.

Around three o'clock in the afternoon, a streak of sun would cover half my bedroom terrace. It was a meager portion, considering that the terrace faced west. But the apartments on the left side of the back building jutted sideways and blocked the sun. It was better than nothing though, and I would sit there, knit, sew, watch the tenants go in and out and the children run around the side lane. Sometimes, Mrs. Zukerman would join me on the terrace, and we would chat until the sun crept to the north and the air grew chilly.

Soon it was March with the smell of spring. Red poppies sprang up between the buildings, in lots and ditches. Gushes of warm breeze blew in, trees flowered, lemon and orange blossoms scented the air, and there was the faint regret that life fell short of anticipation. On my terrace the sun stayed longer and the sparrows hopped about the railing. I would linger there and Mrs. Zukerman would join me for a cup of coffee. Then she would smoke a cigarette. "Not more than three a day," she would say. "I better enjoy the little time left for me in this world."

She also liked clothes: tight sweaters and flowery dresses. Whenever she bought something, she would bring it over to show me, beaming with delight. "I love to spend money," she would tell me. "I will never ever think of tomorrow. When I left the concentration camp I swore I would enjoy every minute of my life."

"And do you?"

"Of course. It's enough that I wake up in the morning, the sun is shining, and I'm not sick. It is enough that I'm among Jews like me, and I don't have to look behind me when I walk down the street."

She took a ritualistic pleasure in smoking her cigarette; she would throw back her head, take a long deep drag, linger on it and puff out the smoke in two or three blasts. She would tell me about the tenants whom she had come to know when she collected the maintenance fees. She would tell me about the Kasmas and how they delayed paying her.

"Listen to what Mr. Kasma told me," Mrs. Zukerman chuckled. "The other day I went to collect maintenance from him. He said he had no money right now but that soon he would pay me for both months. 'What are ten liras a month, Mr. Kasma?' I asked him. 'Do you mean to tell me that you really don't have it?' 'Yes, I really don't have it. Your country doesn't leave my kind any money.' Notice, Mr. Kasma said, 'my kind.' And 'your country,'" Mrs. Zukerman laughed. "As if Israel is mine, not his."

I didn't know what to say. It was no secret that the Sephardic Jews were bitter about discrimination in jobs, education and the like. But I was her "wise and intelligent" person, aware of the other side's claim that most discrimination was only in the mind, while the rest was the natural consequence of a cultural gap which the government was trying so hard to eliminate. Anyway, Mrs. Zukerman could not be personally blamed for discrimination, real or imagined, and I almost felt like apologizing for Mr. Kasma. But Mrs. Zukerman was laughing and I recalled that she had so much understanding of human failings that nothing surprised her. She once told me about an inmate at the concentration camp who would snatch food from her whenever they went to eat, and Mrs. Zukerman had been afraid to complain for fear that justice would prove much worse than the crime. Lately she had come face to face with that woman in a grocery store in Tel Aviv.

"I felt like confronting her and shaming her," Mrs. Zukerman said. "You don't know the atrocities we went through. But we were both Jewish, in the same hell, so I expected better from her. I suppose that in such a horrible struggle for survival, people cannot help becoming inhuman. Also, the woman is much bigger than I, maybe she needed more than that miserable food ration. So I pretended I didn't recognize her and went on my way. I'm sure she remembered me and I wonder what she felt. Not that I mind Mr. Kasma delaying the money," Mrs. Zukerman went on, "but going back and forth for the maintenance money and taking care of the expense account takes a lot of time."

It seemed that Mr. Shamash also delayed paying the maintenance money. Man of the world or not, here was one way in which he resembled Mr. Kasma.

"I went to him," Mrs. Zukerman laughed, "And I said, 'Why don't you give me the money and get it over with? Otherwise, I'll come by every day.' 'That's what I would love most, Mrs. Zukerman,' he said grinning at me."

Two weeks later she described how he finally handed her the money.

"'Mr. Shamash,' I told him, 'next month is almost due. I would like to ask you for the money now that I'm here, but I'm afraid you won't sleep at night.' 'I love not to sleep at night, Mrs. Zukerman,' he said."

Time had a way of slipping by unnoticed. Two years had elapsed. One of the tenants had sold his apartment after his company transferred him to Haifa; another received a big inheritance and moved into a larger apartment.

"I wish I could move too," said Mrs. Kasma. "One bedroom is not enough. There's hardly space to breathe. But we lost money, the store, and the Israeli lira keeps sinking."

That same day I heard a loud commotion outside, and soon Ariel rushed in with the details. Mr. Kasma's grandson had been playing ball on the sidewalk, outside Mr. Shamash's store. Suddenly he hit the glass door. The glass did not break and Mr. Shamash chased him away. But the boy came back and kept on playing. Mr. Shamash went out and hit him. The boy's father was at the Kasma's. He confronted Mr. Shamash and they came to blows. Mr. Shamash called the police.

Next morning, taking Ariel to kindergarten, I saw Mr. Kasma on the sidewalk. He stood and waited for me.

"Did you hear what Shamash, may God erase his name, did yesterday? Why didn't he call us before he hit the boy? If we had been Ashkenazim and not Iraqis like him, would he have dared?"

Two months later Mr. Shamash sold his store to an accountant. "There's not much business here," he told me. "I'll be better off in a busier area."

Mrs. Zukerman provided me with some details about the store's sale one afternoon as she came to join me on the terrace.

"You know what?" she said. "Yesterday I went to the closing of Mr. Shamash's store. A member of the house committee has to sign the consent to the sale."

"I know."

"But listen to this. I asked Mr. Shamash for a hundred liras, as a gift for the building before I signed."

"Really? But you didn't get a gift from the other two tenants who sold their apartments."

"No, I didn't. Some houses do charge for the service. We don't. Anyway Mr. Shamash fell for it. He probably thought it was the procedure here, or perhaps he got a good price for the store, so he really didn't care."

I couldn't help thinking that she had mistreated Mr. Shamash, making him give a gift while exempting the two Ashkenazi tenants who had previously sold their apartments.

It seemed that his smoothness, his making her feel every inch a woman did not go far for him.

"Now listen to this," Mrs. Zukerman interrupted my thoughts. "It is so funny, really." She chuckled. "Just now I met Mr. Kasma and I told him about Mr. Shamash's hundred liras. 'See how I cornered him,' I said. 'Good, good, I am very happy,' he said. 'How can you say that? He is an Iraqi like you,' I teased. You know what he answered? And I swear in all earnest; I don't think he was aware of the implications for me. 'You call this one Iraqi?' he said. 'He's twenty years in this country. He's worse than an Ashkenazi.'"

The Crossroad

"She is not for you, Naiim." His aunt shook her head. "This is Israel, not Baghdad. A seventeen-year-difference!"

She stood by the kerosene lamp, her head bent over the coffee pot. He watched her small, aged body, the grey head sunk between the shoulders, the flat chest, the inflated belly.

He resented her tone. Mild, calm, with distinct finality, typical of someone with an undisputed reputation for wisdom. "Aunt Zebeda is very wise"; the family had given its verdict a long, long time ago.

She lifted the coffee pot off the kerosene lamp, lowered the flame and blew it out. Then she poured the coffee into two demitasse cups, set them on the kitchen table, pulled up a chair and sat in front of him.

"She has a Middle Eastern background," he began lamely.

"Turkish. And Turkish women were always more outgoing than the Iraqi. But what difference does it make? Look at our own Iraqi girls. They're outdoing the Ashkenazim. I see them walking the streets, holding hands with young boys, even hugging them. You are serious and respectable. . . ."

"I wish you would meet Esther," he interrupted. "She is so decent and modest. She comes from a conservative family. Her father

109

wouldn't let her join the army, and she hardly goes out. She has a full-time job, and all she does when she comes home is take care of her father and brother. She really is very modest."

"This country destroys all modesty in women. You heard how that Zilka woman threw her husband out of the house. Think about it. The girl is nineteen and you are thirty-six. It would have been all right in Baghdad. But here, women are as old as their husbands, even older, sometimes."

"She knows about the difference in our ages and she said she doesn't feel it at all. That's what she said."

His aunt would not answer and they drank their coffee in silence.

"Thank you for the coffee," Naiim said. "I have to run to the store now. *Shalom*, aunt." He left.

Maybe he should have had his aunt meet Esther. He himself had first met her when he visited the Maabarah—the immigrant camp—of Raananah. He had gone there at the urgent request of the Shullmans, his friends at the Mapai Center. He had joined the Mapai Party a year ago, hardly a month after he landed in Israel. His uncle, who had been in the country since 1938, strongly recommended it.

"You don't know this country," his uncle had said. "And if you want influential connections, if you want to advance, join a party, any party, but preferably Mapai. It's the strongest, the ruling party."

Naiim joined Mapai and regularly attended the meetings at the Center. It was there that he made friends with the Shullmans. Mr. Shullman held an administrative position in the party, while his wife worked for the Welfare Department. They were a middle-aged couple with a married son in the Kibbutz and a younger one, a bachelor, in the army. Unlike some Ashkenazim, they were neither snobbish nor tactless, but warm and friendly. They took a genuine interest in Naiim, his background, his family. They felt sorry for his brother who still lived in Baghdad, among Arabs, and shook their heads on learning that his two sisters resided in England.

"Tell them to come to Israel," they would say. "It's the only place for Jews."

It was a warm July afternoon when the Shullmans hurried into his grocery shop, told him about the disturbances at the Maabarah and asked for his help.

"Please come with us. You should know how to talk to the immigrants," Mr. Shullman said. "Calm them down. You're their fellow countryman. They'll listen to you."

It was four-thirty. He had just opened his store after the noon break and his assistant was due in an hour's time. Some bread loaves were left over, and he arranged them on the counter. "You two go first. I will soon follow," he said, putting his hand on his chest by way of reassurance. "As soon as my assistant gets here, I'll take the bus and join you."

But the Shullmans insisted on waiting for him in the store. He suspected they did not trust him and he assured them that putting one's hand on one's chest was as good as a written contract and that, back in Baghdad, many important transactions were conducted that way.

"Of course, we trust your word," Mrs. Shullman said. "But it's just easier for you to come with us in the jeep than to wait hours for the bus." She urged him to send for the assistant who, luckily, was home and could come to the store right away.

Naiim went with the Shullmans to the jeep. He watched as Mr. Shullman leaned back in the driver's seat, in full control of the car. His driving was smooth, effortless, the turns sharp but swift and easy. Ashkenazim were so able and efficient. Mr. Shullman was of average height, well-built, muscular, with a large face, small blue eyes and a relaxed expression. Mrs. Shullman was tall with delicate features and fine grey hair. Usually quiet and gentle, she now was excited and anxious, her emotions blurring her words.

The sun was sinking. It was still hot but there was a flow of cool air and Naiim noted a certain smell, familiar yet hard to identify. Then he remembered. Baghdad on the brink of autumn, with the holiday air of Rosh Hashanah and Yom Kippur.

The road was paved, with flat dry land on both sides of it. Army vehicles passed by and, at the turn of the road, a group of giggling young scouts waved *Shalom*. Naiim waved back and thought about the scouts' happy situation. The joy of youth in one's own country, sheltered from the rigors of a Diaspora. Mr. Shullman discussed the disturbances at the Maabarah and claimed that parties, opponents of Mapai, were inciting the immigrants against the government. When he hinted at the irresponsibility of the immigrants, Naiim rushed to the defense of his countrymen. They were honest, decent people, used to better conditions, and living in a tent was not their chosen mode of life.

"I understand but. . . ." And Mr. Shullman embarked on a long speech, stressing the need for cooperation, self-sacrifice for the sake of the ultimate goal, the future of Israel. He himself had seen worse times, and what about the early immigrants who had to struggle against the swamps, malaria, the hostile British and the treacherous Arabs? "Right now, Israel is experiencing great difficulties in settling the immigrants," he said. "A small poor country, daily absorbing such large numbers of people. Is there any wonder that conditions are not the best?"

The jeep stopped at the army supply center, a small building on the main road, a quarter of a mile from the Maabarah. The Shullmans approached the supervisor, a woman in her late fifties, and asked about the situation at the Maabarah.

"Right now it's quiet," she said. "But something is brewing. Some inciters are planning a demonstration."

It was then that he saw Esther. She came to the supervisor with a list of names and a pile of food-stamp booklets. He noted her slim figure, chestnut hair and small sharp features. She did not strike him as really pretty. There was nothing special about her eyes, the one feature that usually enticed him. Hers were small, round, shiny black. Yet for fun, or out of habit, he gave her his look, an intense, unrelenting look which unmistakably declared his interest. She acknowledged his gaze, then lowered her eyes, and at that moment a strange, warm tenderness filled his heart.

"How many new immigrants will arrive today?" Mr. Shullman asked.

"Fifty or fifty-five," the supervisor answered.

"Do you have enough tents?"

"Yes."

"Enough food stamps?"

"Yes."

The Shullmans and Naiim took leave of the supervisor and headed for the Maabarah. Mr. Shullman had parked his jeep on the main
road and the three of them walked the quarter of a mile of unpaved
road leading to the Maabarah, passing forty to fifty tents. It was quiet
except for the faint sound of people talking together and the shrill
voices of children who were roaming between the tents.

Soon it became clear that a meeting was taking place near one of
the tents. Naiim and the Shullmans rushed over. About forty people
were gathered around a tall, bulky man who was apparently presiding over the meeting. He was about thirty years old, with a round
face and big bulging eyes. He spoke animatedly in Arabic. ". . . and
these are the impossible conditions of the Maabarah. . . ."

"Shaoul," someone called to him, motioning toward the Shullmans.

Shaoul shrugged and turned his attention to some cartoon placards printed both in English and Arabic: "We ask the Jordanian government for asylum."

"We will carry white flags and march to the borders," Shaoul said.
"The Arabs cannot be more heartless than these Jews." He took a large
white cloth and tore it in pieces which he distributed to his audience.

"But where is the reporter?" a woman called. "He should have
been here an hour ago."

Naiim could not suppress a smile. Did Shaoul really think he would
go to Jordan, or were the placards just for show at the demonstration,
a desperate attempt to draw the attention of the authorities? Meanwhile, no reporter showed up. Glancing at the Shullmans, Naiim felt
ashamed of his countrymen, not for their anger at their conditions,
nor their inability to surmount difficulties, but for those ridiculous
placards. Jordan for asylum, indeed!

"What are your grievances? Can we discuss it calmly?" Naiim
called to Shaoul in Arabic.

"Yes. Can we know the nature of your grievances?" Mr. Shullman asked in Hebrew.

"Oh really! You really want to know the nature of our grievances?" Shaoul mocked in broken Hebrew. "Or do you want to laugh at us? For months we have been crying out our grievances. And every now and then someone like you comes to make a report. Then nothing!"

"Why don't you listen to him?" Naiim ventured in Arabic and immediately became the target of Shaoul's sarcasm.

"A lawyer!" Shaoul roared. "They hired themselves an Iraqi lawyer!"

"I'm on your side, believe me," Naiim said, again in Arabic. "I just recently left the Maabarah."

"New immigrants!" someone called, and everyone rushed out to look at the newcomers. Naiim and the Shullmans followed.

The new immigrants, forty men, women and children, approached slowly. They looked lost and bewildered. The men wore tailored suits; the women silk dresses, nylon stockings and dainty high-heeled shoes. Naiim smiled sadly. He remembered his own emigration. He remembered the scorching heat at Baghdad's airport verandah, with policemen and guards all around. Since clothes were all one could take and the weight allowance was so limited, he, like his fellow immigrants, had carried his coat and jacket over his arm. As he stood looking aimlessly about, a policeman shouted at him. "You sit down, you with the coat. Trembling from cold, for sure."

The immigrants struggled with their luggage. Feet sinking in the sand, they bent down and pushed the heavy trunks, their coats and jackets dragging along. Reaching the tents, they stopped to catch their breath and were smothered by relatives, friends and acquaintances.

"Where are your beds and blankets?"

"We left them on the road," the immigrants said. "Too heavy to carry. We'll sleep on the ground . . . or the trunks. . . ."

"Oh, no. You'll get sick. This is Israel, not Baghdad. It's damp and chilly at night. We'll go back with you and help you get them."

Soon the commotion around the new immigrants subsided and the people returned to the placards and gathered around Shaoul.

"Now, when we start marching . . . ," Shaoul began.

"Wait, please," Naiim called and walked toward Shaoul.

"What?" Shaoul snapped; the others began shouting.

"Let's hear about your grievances," Naiim said.

"We already . . ."

"I know. Just one more time, please."

"Yes, please," Shullman echoed in Arabic.

The grievances began pouring on Naiim and the Shullmans, in Arabic and mostly in broken Hebrew: The immigrants were being dropped far off from the Maabarah; they were given narrow folding steel beds, thin straw mattresses, flannel blankets and then left to themselves. Most of them had small children and it was an ordeal to carry the luggage, the bedding and the children too.

The Maabarah was practically in the desert; scorpions and snakes were in the deep sand. "So we have to carry the children on our shoulders all the time," the mothers and grandmothers said. "And they keep crying. They're used to the cradles in cool basements with electric fans." Meanwhile, the necessities of everyday living were not available: the milkman, the bread man, the waterman and the gas-man came if and when they pleased, and if one needed something in between one had to take that long walk to the bus station and then wait and wait for the bus. Getting rations from the grocery was as bad. The grocer had only one song: "No delivery yet." Whether it was true or whether he was a swindler, the immigrants had to go back and forth for their rations.

Naiim found himself siding with the immigrants and urging Mr. Shullman to provide the necessary remedies. He came to realize that he himself had been quite lucky. In Maabarat Shaar Alia where he had stayed for a month, conditions had been far better. Meals of dairy products, vegetables and cereals—no meat, poultry, fish or eggs— had been served regularly, and though the quality was poor and the quantity limited, they were sufficiently available nonetheless.

The immigrants went on complaining. The fifty pounds sterling per person allowed by the Iraqi government was melting down, while the few jobs were available only in heavy construction or road work.

Mr. Shullman took center stage at the discussion. He promised he would personally see to it that services were regularly provided, and if there was any way of transporting the new immigrants nearer to the Maabarah, it would certainly be done. As to jobs, he would do all he could to provide them, but he stressed that whatever was available should be welcomed; all work is respectable, none demeaning. Jews had always had a poor opinion of all manual work, but those were old-fashioned, snobbish Diaspora values; here, in Israel, the attitude was completely different. The return to the homeland should encompass a love for the land and all that contributed to its development and growth. Israel would become an advanced agricultural-industrial country, a robust and healthy nation, where manual and intellectual work would be equally essential and equally appreciated. He concluded with what had become the country's slogan: "Patience, it will be good."

"And I assure you that Mr. Shullman will keep his promise," Naiim added and was immediately drowned out by the immigrants who all spoke at the same time, detailing their ordeals.

Naiim could see Mr. Shullman talking with Shaoul and tapping him on the shoulder, while Mrs. Shullman held a friendly conversation with the women. It was quite surprising how quickly the tension had been diffused, to the relief of the Shullmans and the immigrants as well, Naiim observed. What cards did they hold? Naiim shook his head as he glanced at those now-ignored placards.

On the way back, Mr. Shullman again stopped at the army supply center. He instructed the supervisor to see that services were regularly provided to the Maabarah, and that he, Mr. Shullman, should be informed about any developments in the situation. As Esther was heading for the bus station, the Shullmans offered her a lift.

"Am I on your way?" she asked demurely.

"Yes, yes," Mr. Shullman answered.

"Even if you are not on our way," Mrs. Shullman said.

Esther smiled, climbed into the jeep and sat in the back, near Naiim. Dusk was setting in with a thrilling chill. Esther wore a sleeveless linen dress, light yellow with tiny, black dots. Her slim neck swayed with the movement of the jeep, and her left hand held onto the front seat for support. A strange excitement seized Naiim. But it was the Shullmans who did all the talking. They deluged Esther with questions which she readily answered. She lived in Maabarat Zakia Alef with her father and brother. Her mother had died of pneumonia two years ago, back in Turkey, and soon afterwards the family emigrated to Israel. Her father occasionally worked as a guard in construction sites and her twelve-year-old brother went to elementary school. Esther had a full-time job at the army supply center, and also took care of the family: shopping, cooking, laundry, all in the difficult conditions of the Maabarah.

The Shullmans were very impressed with Esther. She was not one of those who "could not understand." They praised her good nature and industriousness and called her "a brave Israeli girl in the true sense of the word." Hard work would always bring good results, they told her, and were coming up with instances illustrating the matter when the jeep suddenly reached Zakia Alef. Esther bade goodbye, jumped off her seat, plunged into the narrow road to the Maabarah and disappeared into the darkness.

A week later, on a Wednesday, when groceries closed for the afternoon, Naiim set out to inspect the situation at the Maabarah. He had previously discussed the matter with Mr. Shullman, who was all approval.

"Very good, really. I am pleased with your sense of responsibility. Keep up the good work and be sure to report everything to me."

At one p.m. during the heat of the day when most people took a noon break, Naiim set out for the Maabarah. He took the ten-minute walk to the bus station and stood waiting, together with some eight people. Luckily the bus came within half an hour, and though it was jammed full, Naiim was able to squeeze himself on the first step and hold on to the front seat railing. The bus passed shabby houses, scattered across a dry, sandy landscape. Naiim got off at the army supply center, looked up Esther and the supervisor, and inquired about the Maabarah situation.

"Everything seems to be all right," the supervisor said.

At the Maabarah, Naiim encountered a different atmosphere from that of his last visit. The angry mood had given way to a gloomy resignation. The necessities were regularly supplied, but jobs were still scarce, and where was the end to life in a tent? There was a distinct reluctance to discuss anything and disenchantment with "Patience, it will be good." The families Naiim encountered had no patience for voicing grievances. The situation was irremediable, too grim for words. Even the usual nostalgic comparisons with Baghdad seemed pointless.

"The Arabs wouldn't have left us alone, anyway," one woman summed it up. "Now that there are so few Jews left in Baghdad, maybe they'll ease up on them."

A few families had received their money from abroad and were preparing to move to an apartment. Others, who had lost everything in the Iraqi freeze of Jewish assets, viewed the situation with desperation.

"Those children rolling in the sand," one man said, "they are used to . . ."

"Stop it, please," his wife snapped. "I can't stand it when you start. . . ."

Naiim spent some time pouring encouragement and hope into deaf ears; then he made his way back to the army supply center.

He arrived in time to accompany Esther to the bus station. She walked with a light step. He paid the fare for both and led her toward the end of the crowded bus. Both held onto the steel railing, and he made sure not to bump into her as the bus swayed back and forth. Bad taste was not his style. Soon a seat was available and Esther sat down. He stood near her, his tall figure bent forward, and had a glimpse of the delicate upper part of her breasts swelling inside her bra. The sight of the smooth olive skin tickled his senses. He told her about his grocery store, his new apartment and furniture.

"You are so lucky," she sighed, and he relished her wishful, dreamy look.

He suggested that she or her father come to his grocery and receive their rations ahead of time, the margarine, eggs and oil.

"That's wonderful," she exclaimed, her eyes sparkling.

Two days later she came to the store. She wore a red cotton dress, buttoned from the middle of the round neck to the hem. She's pretty, Naiim thought. Red heightened the shiny blackness of her eyes and gave a rosy color to her olive skin. He felt a strong urge to touch her neck with his palm. She asked whether it was difficult to transfer the ration books. Not at all, he answered.

There were no customers in the store so he rushed to the back, put a dozen eggs and three margarine bars in a bag and brought them to her.

"I don't want anyone to see," he said, "because I haven't gotten the rations for the month. This is an advance."

"Thank you so much." She blushed. "We didn't even get all of last month's rations."

"I know, I know how it is."

"Is it possible to get a jar of Turkish coffee from the black market?" she ventured shyly.

He promised to bring her one early next week and insisted on giving her some of his own coffee for the time being.

"Thank you very much," she said. "My father will be so happy."

He watched her rosy blush and smiled. "No problem about the ration books," he repeated. "You're in my zone. Just go to the local citizen's office and have them transferred."

Three days later, Esther's father came to the store. He looked to be in his early fifties, rather short with small features and a sly look. His black hair curled at the ends, as did his Charlie Chaplin moustache.

"I went to the registration office but they told me. . . ." And he related his difficulties with the ration transfer in minute detail.

"Let me see." Naiim interrupted to examine the ration books. "I'll give you an advance, a few margarine bars, and by the end of the week I might get some eggs. Esther or you can drop by."

"Thank you, thank you very much." The man's eyes beamed. He slipped the bars into a cloth bag and lingered about the store. Talkative and inquisitive, he leaned on the counter and, between customers, chatted with Naiim.

"You're lucky to own a grocery store," he told Naiim. "I didn't think it was easy for a Sephardi to get a license."

"I didn't get the license myself. I bought the store from an Ashkenazi who had to sell because of his heart condition."

"Well, you're lucky you brought money with you."

Soon Esther's father inquired about Naiim's living quarters, and when he heard it was not a tent or a hut but a normal two-bedroom apartment in Houlon, his eyes danced with excitement.

"Wonderful! You're lucky to have taken some money out of Baghdad."

The apartment was not furnished, Naiim said, but it would be soon. He was expecting money from the sale of his car by his brother back in Baghdad. In 1951, Naiim explained, the Iraqi government issued a laissez-passer permit allowing Jews to leave the country, for Israel only, on condition that they gave up their Iraqi citizenship, including all rights. Naiim opted for the laissez-passer, but before registering he transferred his car's ownership to his brother who did not register. The precaution paid off. Others in Naiim's position had trusted the Iraqi government because it allowed those who registered early to sell their belongings, and then suddenly they were hit by a decree freezing all their assets.

"Very smart," Esther's father said. "Why don't you come over to our place on Saturday? So we can chat a little."

"I'll see. . . ."

"Do you have anything to do on Saturday?"

"No."

"Then come. You know where Maabarat Zakia Alef is. We're in the fifth hut in the second row."

"I'll come. Ten-thirty, eleven."

"Good. We'll drink coffee and chat. By the way, is it possible to get some coffee?"

"Oh, yes, I got your jar. I completely forgot about it."

Naiim went to the back of the store. He smiled, thinking of the way Esther's father had brought up the subject of the coffee. He, Naiim, had not forgotten about it. But it was not his policy to pour too many favors down anyone's throat in one single shot. He had been in business for many years and had dealt with people long enough to know that such a practice did more harm than good. A little at a time would keep all parties content and well-disposed toward each other. Naiim spent the week in euphoric anticipation. Esther's sparkling eyes and smooth olive skin haunted him in endless situations and episodes; she was his demure fiancée, and he held her tenderly, her slim limbs pressing against his body; she was his lawful wife and he made love to her with the delicacy of romance and the vigor of passion; she was the devoted mother of his children and he hovered protectively over her and their little ones. He smiled indulgently at his racing thoughts. When toying with hopeful situations and getting carried away, he often checked himself for fear of disappointment. But this time he let the reins loose. Let hope thrive while it could.

Saturday morning at nine-thirty, Naiim set out for the road. It was a half-hour walk to the entrance of the Maabarah. He wore his beige gabardine slacks, a white shirt and brown leather shoes. He had been in Israel for a year, but he could not get used to wearing sandals. They looked all right on Ashkenazim, but not on him. Sandals clashed with his notion of respectability.

There was no public transportation on Saturday, so Naiim planned to hitchhike. Everyone did, so why shouldn't he? The road, glowing in bright sunlight, was deserted. Two army vehicles drove by, ignoring Naiim's wave. They were not supposed to stop for civilians, but he knew that they often did. A jeep with jubilant young people dressed for the beach sped by. It was full and Naiim did not wave. Soon another jeep stopped and the driver, a young Ashkenazi man, offered Naiim a lift.

"A new immigrant?" the young man asked.

"I've been here for almost a year now."

A friendly conversation ensued. The young man, twenty-three years old, was fair with small gray eyes, curly blond hair and an engaging smile. He wore a white T-shirt, blue shorts and biblical sandals. And he had a wife and two children. Twenty-three years old and already with a family! The thought weighed on Naiim's chest. He himself was so far behind. But it was only here in Israel that he had come to realize it. Back in Baghdad, most men married when they were over thirty; they had to acquire the money before they could go about raising a family. Here, men could get married and live in one rented room in a shared apartment.

"There you are. Zakia Alef."

"Thank you very much," Naiim said.

"You are welcome."

Naiim crossed the street and entered the narrow unpaved road leading to the Maabarah. The urgency to get married disturbed him. He disliked urgency in anything. It made one nervous, put one therefore at a disadvantage and prone to make a mistake. That was why it had been his practice to make early provisions, to be always ahead of time. In this case he had been neglectful. He had often thought about marriage back in Baghdad. But with good Sabina catering to his needs, and the turmoil of the laissez-passer, he had not considered it seriously. He had never felt that time was running out except this last year in Israel. Just a while ago he had jokingly declared his interest in an Ashkenazi girl who was no younger than twenty-four, and she had immediately rebuffed him. "You're really handsome, but too old for me."

The customers who came to his store seemed to think the same way. "You should get married, and soon," one customer told him. "You don't want to have your children feeling they have an old man for a father?" It was no surprise, for the country was full of men in their early twenties, almost boys, who were husbands and fathers. And the way they spoiled their children. All Jewish parents cared for their children, but here, they carried pampering too far.

"What do I need money for? Why do I need anything?" the gas man once told Naiim. "When I take my boys for a walk on a Sabbath, I feel like a Rothschild."

The Sabbath family walk was a national ritual. Late winter mornings and early summer evenings were the scheduled times when dressed-up parents and children went for their walk. The holiday dress of the children was a white shirt, with a blue skirt for the girls, and blue pants for the boys, the two colors of the Israeli flag.

As Naiim approached the huts, he smelled red-poached eggs. There must be some Iraqis in the Maabarah; who else cooked eggs that way? With all the hardships and the scarcity of eggs, they managed to maintain their traditional Sabbath morning meal. Naiim remembered with regret the lavish Sabbath winter brunches back in Baghdad. The red poached eggs, the chicken, its skin stuffed with meat, its soup cardamom-flavored, all with the special taste of overnight cooking on low heat; while here was the aura of deprivation; deprivation of food, clothing, housing; even the air smelled of deprivation.

"Good morning," Esther's father greeted Naiim and let him into the four-by-five wooden hut. Three narrow high risers were set against its walls, with a steel trunk under each one of them. At the entrance, by the tiny window, wooden shelves were set on bricks, serving as a counter for a few dishes, two pots and a kerosene lamp. A small wooden table and two chairs stood in the middle.

Naiim extracted two chocolate bars from his pocket, one for Esther, one for her twelve-year-old brother. Esther unwrapped the bar and offered it. Naiim refused. "I can get as many as I want," he found himself boasting.

"The black market?" Esther's father asked.

"Yes," Naiim answered and immediately changed the subject. He did not care to indulge the man's inquisitiveness. "It's good you have a wooden hut," he said.

"We of Zakia Alef," Esther's father retorted, "have stayed so long in tents that they knew it was right to give us the wooden hut, not the tin one. You should have seen us last winter during the flood, the mud to our knees."

Naiim noted the rebuke in the man's tone and chose to ignore it. "I know, I know," he said.

"You don't have these problems, you . . ."

"You're right." Naiim smiled. "I didn't say it was easy. I just meant a wooden hut is better than a tin one. How about the water?"

"The water van comes more often now, but . . ." Esther's father went on complaining about the difficulty of transportation, the scarcity of jobs, the lack. .... He prepared Turkish coffee for Naiim while talking about his past, his present, his children. He talked about Esther and how he would like to see her settled, not with one of those hollow youngsters, but with a decent, solid person, a person of character. Naiim noted Esther's blush. He watched her, her father, her brother, and decided that it would be up to him if and when he proposed.

A few days later, Esther came for the rations, and Naiim gave her an advance on the eggs and the margarine.

"You don't have to. I can wait," she protested.

"It's all right."

As she lifted the carton of eggs, he touched her fingers. She did not withdraw her hand, but lowered her eyes and blushed. He smiled at her bashful confusion, her clumsiness as she hurriedly put the eggs and margarine in the handbag, thanked him and left.

The relationship progressed. Naiim became a constant visitor at Esther's place. He invited the family to his apartment and took Esther out several times. It was then that he decided to inform his aunt; after all, she was his closest relative in Israel. Her strong objections surprised him and shook his composure.

He recovered. She did not know the whole picture. He would have to explain it to her in detail. He had had similar doubts at one time, because, as he came to know Esther better, he began noticing some flightiness about her. Sometimes, she indulged in giggling fits with her brother, and she liked to go out a lot. Naiim did not know whether to attribute her behavior to her age or to her character. He conveyed his hesitancy to her father who dismissed it as unfounded. What Naiim described, the father said, was the outward aspect of Esther's character; in reality, she was a good, decent and sensible girl, mature for her age, and he gave many examples of that. Naiim readily bought the explanation, acknowledging that, to Esther's credit, she really took good care of her family. And what choice did he have? An Ashkenazi girl with loose morals was out of the question, while the Iraqi girls had readily adopted the Israeli same-age formula. The prospect of marrying a withered thirty-year-or-older woman with a sagging body, completely turned him off. However, sure of his grounds, he broached the subject of age with Esther.

"I don't feel it," she said. "My father told me what you said, but I don't feel it."

He was pleased with her answer. Most Iraqi men were married to younger women, and there was nothing wrong with their marriages. And he was a handsome man. Tall, well-built, with strong features. He could see it in the eyes of women, especially the Ashkenazi ones who were far from bashful. There was the divorcee, Deborah, blond and cute, who invited him to her apartment for coffee; "no commitment," she had joked. But he wanted no entanglement with a thirty-five-year-old woman who also had a child. He discussed Ashkenazi women with Esther. He told her how he disapproved of their loose ways and was pleased to hear that she shared his opinion. She was a modest and sensible girl.

The marriage took place in early fall and proved to be more of a blessing than Naiim had anticipated. Esther's velvet pale skin and slender limbs did wonders for his sexual desire; her warm response and the way she cuddled into his embrace were most rewarding.

Esther was very proud of her new apartment. She kept it clean, tidy, and took great pains to complete its furnishing, piling up household items like table pads, kitchen towel-hooks . . . which Naiim did not think he needed or cared for. But the apartment acquired a warm, lovely atmosphere. Esther knew how to cook well, having catered to her family ever since her mother died. And when Naiim got ready to go home for lunch or dinner, the prospect of the good meal, Esther's shapely limbs and the cozy apartment filled him with complacent anticipation. Meanwhile, he was doing very well at the store. The rations and the black market were full of opportunities and he had learned the ins and outs of the business from the former store owner.

What added to the bliss was that soon Esther became pregnant— the arrival of a child, God willing a male, promised more joy and happiness. But what somehow marred the bliss was that Esther's father had turned the couple's nest into his first, rather than his second home. Always out of work, through necessity or lack of motivation, he would come to hang around Esther, keep her company and enjoy her cooking. Naiim did not offer a warm welcome, but the father didn't seem to mind, especially since he timed most of his visits when Naiim was at the store. "How can he leave your brother alone and come all the way here?" Naiim asked Esther. "My brother is at school," she answered. "And he stays there even after school hours."

The father did not forsake his son's company all the time. On Saturdays, he made sure to bring him along to visit Esther from early morning till night. Naiim mentioned her father's shortcomings to Esther. "Tell him not to lie on the sofa without putting a sheet on it. Tell him not to lean on the walls with his hands each time he moves about the apartment. His sweaty fingers will stain the walls."

It was not that Naiim was stingy or unkind; he just believed in maintaining things in their right measure, which end he accomplished by having Esther help him at the store. It was an altogether good move, since his assistant was not without his faults, and there was nothing better than managing one's own business. "Tend to your goat," as the saying went, "and it would bear twins." And Esther would benefit from leaving the house, as a change of surroundings, while her father would stick to his own place, an empty house not being much of an incentive for his visits. It was then that her father suggested he would be most willing to help at the store. But Naiim was adamant. Family members should not get involved in business. A wife was a different matter. And the customers were delighted with Esther. "So cute, so pretty," they would say, "so warm and friendly." Naiim also decided not to stay home every Saturday, but to go out to visit his aunt or the nearby amusement park, at least every other week. Meanwhile he saw to it that Esther did not exert herself either in the house or the store. He was concerned about her welfare and the baby's.

A baby boy, big and healthy, was born in late summer and was named David, after Naiim's father. Naiim was most happy. Soon, though, he became concerned. He noticed that Esther was negligent in caring for the baby. She let him cry a lot, didn't change him often enough and didn't dress him warmly. Was she young or just frivolous? So he conducted a vigilant watch on how she fed him, bathed him or put him to bed. He helped her as much as he could and hired a woman to clean the house. He wished Esther's father would make frequent visits as he had before, in order to help Esther. But by now the man had a full-time job in a factory, and though he seemed to love the baby, he hardly had time for him.

Naiim pointed out to Esther her shortcomings as a mother, but instead of complying and reforming, she grumbled and sulked. One thing she was bent on doing properly, though—taking the baby out for fresh air once or twice a day. She would dress him, put him in the carriage and walk to the nearby park—rather a small one with a few benches, seesaws and slides. People frequented the park to enjoy the fresh air and warm sun, and Esther brought back advice about the baby, nonsense talk and gossip. There was the time when one woman told her not to pick up the baby when he cried. Otherwise, she would set a pattern. Babies loved to be picked up and often used their crying to manipulate their parents and become spoiled. So it followed that one day Naiim came home to find the baby choking-blue from crying, and Esther minding her own business.

"Are you crazy?" he shouted.

There followed a big argument and though Esther defended her theory, from then on she did not carry it that far.

Then there was the clothes issue. Someone had told Esther to dress the baby lightly so that he would develop resistance to the rigors of cold weather. Naiim objected, in vain. But when the baby developed one cold after another, he raised a commotion, complained to her father who sided with him, and Esther had to change her ways.

"Do you know that people can't believe I'm David's mother?" Esther told him one day. "They think I'm his sister or a baby-sitter."

"They like to tease you," Naiim replied. Maybe not. He watched her brown hair drawn back in a pony tail , her smooth tender skin and its velvet touch. Perhaps she really looked younger than her age. He liked her slender neck, her long limbs, making her seem taller than five foot three. She would go about the apartment, tending to her housework in quick, jerky movements, with the swiftness of a deer and the impulsiveness of a tomboy. She was pretty, and a hard-working girl in the bargain. It was just that she was so talkative. She would not let go of the neighbors or they would not let go of her, whichever; the result was continuous chatter up and down the stairway, at the doorways or through the terraces. He especially resented her encounters with the milkman and the gas man. She would lunge so close to them, almost throwing herself at them, her delicate breasts moving under her thin dress. And the result was that she neglected her duties. Once he asked her to sew a button for his Saturday shirt, but when Saturday came the shirt was still without a button.

"Couldn't you have done it earlier? You've had it since Monday."

"Don't you dare shout at me!" she flared.

A quarrel followed and Naiim complained to her father.

"She has a lot to do." The father sided with Esther this time. "It's not easy to raise a child. And Esther is so young, she's a child herself."

What kind of talk was that? If a girl was old enough to marry, she was old enough to take care of a family.

One day, Esther came home with the story that the mailman had mistaken Naiim for her father; another day she repeated the comment of the gas man: "Where did your husband pick such a flower?"

Naiim was quite annoyed. He abhorred such talk. It smelled of lechery. What business had any man to utter such nonsense unless he had some low purpose in mind?

"All they want is to flatter a woman and make her lose her head," Naiim said and scolded Esther for allowing or perhaps encouraging such behavior.

But harsh words or even quarrels did not last long. There was the coziness of the apartment, the warmth of the bed, Esther's jolly nature, Naiim's protective attention, and then there was David, almond-eyed and with such a sweet mouth. A beautiful, lively child! In the evenings, when Naiim and Esther took him out for a walk, people would stop and admire. And Naiim hardly ever left him with a babysitter. There was no problem when the neighboring couple, by now friends, visited in the evenings. But when reciprocation was due, Naiim made sure to go up and check on David at least every forty-five minutes. David was fourteen months old when Esther became pregnant again. Soon afterward, her father married Marcelle, a childless widow of Iraqi origin. Marcelle and Naiim took to each other from the beginning. They had their hometown, Baghdad, in common.

"She's a very pleasant woman," Naiim told Esther.

"My father is pleasant too."

Marcelle had a dark complexion, a large pleasant face, kind eyes and even teeth. She worked as a seamstress in Ramat-Gan and had her own one-bedroom apartment. As soon as the father moved in with Marcelle, Esther began urging that they too move to Ramat-Gan. What made her suggestion understandable if not reasonable was that Naiim's store was not doing that well. Gone were the days of rations and the black market when a grocery store owner was a king. Austerity was no longer a mode of life. Rations, long bus queues and unemployment, though not the Maabarot, had gradually disappeared, and a grocery store became a source of modest, hard-earned income. What made matters worse was that a new "shekem" store opened across the street, just a few stores from Naiim's. The "shekem" was intended for army men and their immediate families, but it was amazing how many relations and friends sneaked in. There was no competing with the government's subsidized prices, and Naiim's business slowed down considerably.

"Perhaps you can open a grocery store in Ramat-Gan," Esther's father kept telling Naiim. "All your hometown people are there."

It was true that Ramat-Gan was full of Iraqis. But it would be the same story everywhere, and Naiim decided that if he were to give up the store he might as well change professions. Maurice, his aunt Zebeda's son-in-law, urged him to do it. He suggested a brokerage partnership, a connection between lenders and borrowers; the country was developing and many such offices were doing very well. Maurice was an officer in a bank and he knew the ins-and-outs of the business world. He recommended two of his acquaintances as partners for Naiim, introduced them to one another, and soon the three of them opened a brokerage office in Ramat-Gan. These were hectic times. The store had to be sold, the new business required much attention, and the baby was due shortly. Naiim was able to manage it all. He sold his apartment and bought a new one in Ramat-Gan. Esther was helpful; so were her father and brother. Naiim and Esther looked forward to a new and happy future.

The new business seemed to be quite promising. The office was on a first floor, a two-room apartment on Jabotinski Street. The two partners, one Iraqi and one Ashkenazi, were capable and congenial. At first, Naiim had objected to opening a business with an Ashkenazi. They were so shrewd and cunning. He remembered the Shullmans and how he had come to mistrust them. It had been after the incident at the Alia construction site when the Iraqi workers, recruited from Maabarat Talpiot, staged a sit-in strike. The Iraqi workers had believed that the small garden apartments they were helping to build were intended for them, and when it came out that the government was going to reserve them for immigrants from Poland, the workers were beside themselves with anger and frustration. However, their protest was suppressed with threats about their jobs.

Naiim, happening to meet Mr. Shullman, asked about the reason for the discrimination.

"I can be frank with you; you are intelligent and understanding about these matters. These Polish immigrants have a choice of remaining in their Diaspora. So we have to induce them to come. And you know how much we need immigrants."

From then on, Naiim wasted no love on Ashkenazim. But his partner, Mr. Butovski, was highly recommended by Maurice. Each of the partners put in an equal and substantial amount of capital. Naiim and his Iraqi partner provided the lenders while Mr. Butovski brought in the borrowers.

"How can it pay to open a business with more than 20% interest?" Naiim asked his Iraqi partner.

"It pays. It pays."

"Then how come our Iraqis don't do it?"

"They don't know their way about it yet. They don't have the right connections. They don't know how and where to get the right concessions, the grants. Haven't you figured it out by now?"

Naiim did know some well-to-do Iraqis who had ventured into big business and had lost a great deal of money. His countrymen seemed better off as employees, with their money earning interest. Meanwhile, friends and acquaintances gradually began bringing in their money, collected interest and, since the transactions were behind the counter, did not pay taxes. The office dealt with good customers only, and in this respect, Maurice was an excellent source of information.

Esther had more than her days full with Rena, the new baby girl. But she adjusted easily to her new environment. The second floor three-bedroom apartment was sunny, airy and its two front terraces overlooked Hibat Sion Street. It was in a central location, close to a shopping center, to public transportation, schools, kindergartens and the government clinic. Esther was more than excited with her new surroundings and she endlessly babbled about the apartment, the neighborhood. . . . Naiim often came home during lunchtime. Rena was a delicate baby and he wanted to be there to help. But Esther seemed to manage quite well. She had a twice-a-week maid for the cleaning and laundry, and she herself was no weakling. Meanwhile Naiim's business was prospering and the future looked bright; the ingredients for happiness were all there.

The neighbors seemed to be congenial, and Esther became especially friendly with Doris, a young woman of Iraqi origin. Soon the two were in and out of each other's apartments, the men on cordial greeting terms. Doris was small with a round face, straight hair and a good smile. She had two little boys, four and three years old, and the two women babysat for each other. It was all so convenient, yet Naiim was uneasy. He came to realize that Doris had too much influence on Esther. She was twenty-eight years old, had been married for seven years and tended to advise Esther on everything from house maintenance to child-raising to husband handling. It annoyed Naiim that in matters concerning his own household it was often Doris's word, not his, that prevailed. What further disenchanted him was the kind of husband Doris had. Yehouda was giddy, almost clownish. He claimed to be in his early thirties, but his hair was more white than black and the skin under his eyes was wrinkled, probably a result of his ever-present, blank, meaningless smile. Yehouda was constantly striving to crack jokes, eyeing Esther and Doris to judge the effect. When Naiim tried to engage him in serious conversation, he seemed disconcerted, restless. Once, however, he became really involved. The subject was the coming election, and Yehouda let out a torrent of heated words, mostly directed at Esther, as though she were the one who had brought up the subject.

"Let the wolves eat each other," Yehouda suddenly broke into a chuckle. "We'd better concentrate on having a good time," and he told a joke, quite an indecent one at that.

Naiim lost no time in telling Esther what he thought of the couple, but she defended them angrily. She went about quoting them, praising their achievements, and urging Naiim to befriend them. Some evenings she would leave the children with him and go to their apartment. Naiim did not want to encourage this behavior, but Esther constantly complained about being tied down with the children, so he decided to let it go for the time being.

Soon Doris gave a party, and invited Esther and Naiim. Naiim was reluctant to go, but Esther insisted and he went. There were five couples there, about Yehouda's and Doris's age, all of Iraqi origin. They gathered outside on the big terrace which extended from the living room to one of the bedrooms. Naiim sat near a tall, balding young man named Jacob, who seemed quite sensible. Naiim talked to him about the old Baghdadi way of doing business, where a word was worth more than a thousand contracts. He described cases in which he or his friends had been involved. The conversation had switched to politics when Yehouda suddenly came over.

"What are you two so excited about?" he asked.

"We're solving the problems of the world," Jacob said, smiling.

"Don't tell me you're taking away the livelihood of those poor politicians, breaking your heads over the world's dilemmas?"

"If you don't care to break your head over the world's dilemmas, maybe others do," Naiim retorted.

"Yes, but not Jacob. There aren't enough brain cells in that thick head of his and I could see he was suffering."

Jacob suddenly turned to Doris. "Your new haircut is very nice. It makes you look like a teenager."

What kind of silly talk was that? What respectable man would comment on the haircut of another man's wife? Naiim told the group about his brother who by now was in London. He mentioned his family, Twaig, and how it was related to the well-known Baghdadi families, but no one seemed to know anything about those families. Where did they come from?

Between the tea, the cookies and the fruit, the men told indecent jokes, roaring with laughter while the women giggled encouragingly.

"Tell us the story about the man. . . ."

"Don't you have anything better to talk about than those filthy jokes?" Naiim asked. "And in front of decent women!"

"Dirty jokes are our bread and butter," Yehouda said.

"Shut up, you fool," a man named Ezra retorted. "He's right. Heed the voice of wisdom, you sinners, and refrain from your frivolity." The mock outrage drew unanimous laughter.

"Imagine telling dirty jokes back in Baghdad!" Ezra went on. "When I see a young boy talking to a young girl here, I get a pain in my chest. We could hardly look at a girl back in Baghdad, let alone talk to her."

Naiim tried to catch Esther's eye and motion to her that it was time to leave, but she was busy chattering with one of the women.

"It is almost twelve," Naiim finally announced. "We'd better go home."

"Already? As early as the chickens? Early to bed, early to rise . . . ," the comments filled the room.

"It's been a long day for me," Naiim apologized, but firmly stood up and headed for the door. Esther followed.

"Let's go to Tel Aviv and walk along the beach," Ezra called to everyone.

"Let's go," a few guests agreed.

"No," others objected. "Tomorrow we take the children to the beach and . . ."

The issue was being debated while Naiim and Esther went through the preliminaries of leave-taking: thank-you and we-enjoyed-it-very-much.

"Disgusting," Naiim commented, once outside the door.

"Shh, wait till we get home."

"Stupidity," Naiim said as soon as they entered their apartment. "How can you enjoy such filth?"

"I don't mind it."

"You liked it. I saw you laughing all the time."

"I couldn't help it. It was so funny. It's just jokes. They don't see anything wrong with it."

"Nothing wrong in anything. Why don't we all take off our clothes and . . ."

Esther was actually taking off her clothes. The dim light of the table lamp cast a shadow on her full, shapely figure. The terrace door was half open and a light breeze cooled the room. With her typical swiftness she was already in her nightgown and under the sheets. She had been so pretty tonight, prettier than all those elaborately made-up women. The few pounds she had retained from her pregnancy gave her a sensuous juicy appeal.

He slipped under the sheets and extended his arms. Impatient apathy welcomed him. He became extra gentle, ardent, and was most pleased with the results.

The next morning, Saturday, Naiim woke up with a headache. It was a clear day and the houses across the street glowed in bright sunlight. Then came the usual morning hassle—Rena to be changed and fed, David coaxed to eat his breakfast, the beds to be made, the table to be cleared. It was already ten o'clock when Naiim finally settled on the terrace and sipped his Turkish coffee.

"Let's go to the beach," Esther said.

Naiim put down his coffee. "David has been coughing all week, and I have a bad headache."

"Then let's go to my father's."

They dressed and walked to her father's apartment. Quiet bliss reigned over the streets. The deafening diesel buses were on holiday; the ever-crowded shops closed, the busy breadwinners lingering in sleep.

Marcelle opened the door, and the smell of red-poached eggs and Turkish coffee filled the air. Esther's father rushed for the children. Naiim settled in a chair and called for attention.

"Let me tell you about Esther's new friends," he began and told all about the night before and the indecent jokes.

"That's what they learn from the Ashkenazim. Disgusting," Marcelle said. "Some Iraqis are really behaving crazy. Trying to be modern and copying the Ashkenazim. The trouble is that they become worse than. . . ."

"Yes," Esther's father agreed. "That's what the Ashkenazim teach. I hear their filthy talk at work." And he went on to complain about his work, a respectable steady job at the bank which Marcelle's cousin had been good enough to secure for him.

Early morning Sunday, Doris came to pick up David for kindergarten. "How did you like my party?" she sang.

"Very nice, great," Esther volunteered while Naiim acted as though he were deaf.

"Everyone thought your wife was charming," Doris said to Naiim.

He ignored her remark, and she took David's hand and led him out of the apartment.

"I would have liked to tell her how I liked her party," Naiim told Esther.

"No, please, Naiim. What are you trying to do?"

But he would not tell Doris anything. It was wiser to maintain a good relationship with neighbors, no matter who they were, and Naiim let it go at that.

Esther began neglecting her duties. When they had first moved in, she was so proud of the new apartment that she kept it spotless, the children sparkling clean. But lately she had been dragging her feet. What annoyed Naiim was that she had a cleaning woman twice a week, and he himself was a big help; he often did the shopping, fed the children, played with them or put them to bed. Naiim suspected that Doris was the cause. The two women spent too much time together, chatting, gossiping or shopping.

"What has Doris got to do with it?" Esther protested when Naiim rebuked her about his laundry.

Harsh words followed; hard feelings ensued. Esther sulked and he became nervous. Speech was kept at a minimum, the atmosphere electrically charged and ready to blow up. Then out of nowhere emerged the climax of reconciliation, a prelude of tender, silky verbal and physical communication.

One of Doris's friends, Mary, was having a party, and she invited Esther and Naiim. Naiim refused to go.

"So we don't mix with anyone except my father and Marcelle?" Esther scowled.

"I don't like these people," Naiim said; he thought that from now on he and Esther should visit his Aunt Zebeda, Cousin Violette and Maurice more often.

"You don't have to like them. It's going out. Nice for a change. What are you losing?" And she finally coaxed him into going.

The party was at Mary's apartment on Herzl Street, an eight-block walk. Naiim dallied with his children, dallied over his dinner, his shower, while Esther waited impatiently. When he and Esther finally arrived at the party, all the guests were already there.

Having gotten over his first shock at the group's strange behavior and their devotion to filthy stories, Naiim began watching them closely. He listened to their chatter and hardly put in a word or question. He just observed. They all seemed to be relatively well off, owning their own apartments in the center of Ramat-Gan. As to their behavior, the men acted like clowns and the women like

spoiled brats. What prompted the men to try to compete and sur-
pass each other in being ridiculous? Naiim could not possibly understand. The women, on the other hand, dressed elaborately, and
wore a lot of make-up. None was really pretty, but each one acted as
though she were a Cleopatra. What puzzled Naiim most was the behavior of one of the women, Dina, in her early twenties, dark, with a
flat nose, thin wild hair and Chinese eyes. She was recently married,
and her husband, Ezra, described some of her mistakes. She ruined
one recipe after another. Once she forgot a pot on the stove, went
to lie down and when the burning smell permeated the place, she
called to ask Ezra whether he had dropped a cigarette somewhere.
It was practically impossible to wake her up once she had gone to
sleep. Coming home, one time, Ezra had to climb in through the
neighbor's terrace because Dina did not hear the doorbell ringing.
Ezra related each of these episodes as though it was some amusing
exploit, while Dina sat back quietly, a half smile on her face, seem-
ing to enjoy the attention. "The retarded brat," Naiim called her,
from then on.

"Monday I will be off to Haifa," Doris announced toward the end
of the party. "Yehouda has a day off and he'll stay with the children."

"I wish I could go too," Esther said.

"Why not?" Doris said. "I'm staying with my aunt. You can join
me."

"Go ahead," Jacob grinned. "Let the Haifans have a good time."

"Let the Haifans have a good time," Naiim snapped. "Just what do
you mean by that?"

"Wouldn't the Haifans have a good time with two pretty women,
two flowers adorning their city?"

"Oh, oh," Doris chanted. "What gallantry. What eloquence."

"Jacob is turning into a poet," Yehouda mocked.

Jacob had cleverly sweetened his remark, but Naiim still smoldered at the impudence, the mere . . . disrespect. As to Doris suggesting that Esther would join her! Yehouda worked for the government;
days off cost him nothing; while Naiim was on his own, and a day off
meant less income.

Naiim let it go. However, once outside the party, he gave full vent to his annoyance.

"'Let the Haifans have a good time.' What kind of nonsense is that? Are the Haifans receiving some whores, or what?"

"Oh, don't make a big fuss about it. He was trying to be funny, that's all."

With such nonsense talk, no wonder these silly women thought they were Cleopatras.

Naiim took Esther and the children to visit his aunt who was spending a few days with her daughter, Violette, in Tel-Ganim. Aunt Zebeda was her usual wise self; Violette had her unmistakable quiet, serene manner, and Maurice was as ever, sharp, knowledgeable and well-informed—no wonder he was already an officer in a bank. Naiim enjoyed Maurice's company, and he could see that the children were having a good time in the backyard. But he was not sure about Esther. She was polite with Aunt Zebeda, she exchanged views about the children with Violette, but she looked distant and withdrawn.

"You seemed bored at Aunt Zebeda's," Naiim asked her later. "Don't you like Violette?"

"Yes, I do. I just had a headache. My God, the way Violette dresses!"

"Very simply. No make-up. Well, she is all for her husband, home and children."

Violette was heavy, with thick legs, and she wore orthopedic shoes. She had large cow eyes, a short flat nose and thick lips. She was not pretty, Naiim acknowledged, but she had a beautiful smile thanks to her straight white teeth, and probably her good nature.

"Doris saw her once," Esther remarked. "She said Violette thinks it won't make much difference whether she takes care of herself or not. So she may as well give the impression that she's plain because she dresses plainly."

Naiim invited his Iraqi partner and his wife to tea. But no social friendship developed. The partner and his wife were poker players and had no interest in anyone outside their own group.

Meanwhile Esther made friends with Doris's crowd, and they invited her and Naiim to their rotating Friday night gatherings. Naiim noticed that in Israel most couples belonged to a clique, usually from the same hometown, and they engaged in joint activities all week long. But it was most apparent on Friday evenings, when by five in the afternoon, all offices, factories and stores were closed. Buses did not operate and even private cars and cabs were reduced to a minimum. The streets were deserted as people prepared for the Sabbath. Then, around eight, adult human traffic resumed, people dressed for the holiday, on their way to homes, movie houses, theaters or night clubs. Naiim kept his earlier feelings about Doris's friends, but they were a clique all right, and he resigned himself to belonging, but with reservations. He joined them here; he refrained from joining them there. They were not good company. The men were, as usual, occupied with vulgar stories, their indecent eyes on the women. No new dress, new shoes or new hairdo would escape their silly, infantile compliments. They would look as though they were in a trance, a stupid, unnatural smile stretching as far as their ears. They were especially attentive to Esther, perhaps because she was the prettiest and youngest. But she was on her guard. She knew that if she did not behave well, he would cut all contact with the group. And he constantly corrected her manner and conduct. He did not want her to giggle or engage in silly talk that would encourage the men.

"Are you jealous?" she asked once.

No, he was not jealous, he retorted, except for her reputation, her good name. She was his wife, she bore his name and she was the mother of his children. He himself did not strike up a friendship with any one of the men in the group. They never cared to listen to what he said, nor did they address him directly. Going to work in the morning, he often met Yehouda and Ezra on the bus, but, except for the greeting and a few words here and there, neither cared to start a conversation with him. But they chattered endlessly with each other and even when they sat apart, they exchanged knowing glances from time to time.

He couldn't care less. His business was doing well. He had installed a telephone at home, bought carpets for the living room and

the hall and presented Esther with a gold bracelet. But Esther was
not a grateful person. With Rena growing up and less work to do,
she became more and more negligent. He knew it was the influence
of Doris and her friends. These idle women were constantly up to
something: the beach in summer, the sunny parks in fall and winter.
And shopping! Naiim began to keep an eye on Esther's expenses, especially after he came upon some money in a drawer. Esther claimed
that she had forgotten about it, but he suspected she wanted to put it
aside. He began asking about purchases and demanded to know why
she wanted more and more every day. She complained about inflation
and sulked. One day, in the middle of a quarrel, he threatened to limit
her expenses unless she changed her ways. They both became silent
and moody and the air smoldered with ill humor. But the next day
necessary contact concerning the children and household dispersed
the clouds, and Esther became more agreeable and devoted to her
duties as wife and mother. Then two days later, out of nowhere, she
came up with the most exasperating remark.

"You cannot limit my expenses as you please," she said. "This is
Israel, not Baghdad. And here, the law forces you to take good care of
me before anything else."

"Which one of the whores told you that?" He blew up. The fact
that it had taken her three days to come up with an answer suggested
that someone else's head was at work.

He could not understand why she was so negligent. He made it
a point to complain to her father, but lately the man lent a deaf ear
while Marcelle always gave a noncommittal answer. And there were
the days when he came home to find his supper half ready, other days
when the children were dirty, the house untidy. To her, cleaning the
house meant whatever the maid did, nothing more, no matter how
the children messed it up. He believed she had been a better cook
when she was a young girl. Now she sometimes bought vegetables
and forgot about them until they rotted in the refrigerator. And it was
not that she was a weakling; she had the devil's strength in her. He
watched her on the days she planned to go to the beach. She would
get up early, prepare breakfast in no time, dress the children, fill the

picnic bag and get ready to go. Her infatuation with the beach often caused the children to be sick.

"What do you expect, with your madness with the beach?"

And whenever the children were sick, she became like a trapped animal. The moment he arrived home, she wanted to be out, to her father, to Doris, anywhere. He let her go to her father or to Doris for a while, but not to join the clique in their outings; it was either with him or not at all. He did put his foot down on important issues, quarrel or no quarrel. The children were delicate and should be taken to the beach only on very warm days. As for roaming around every night, he was not a millionaire who could afford an all-week babysitter. She should be thankful she had a well-to-do husband. This was Israel, where some people struggled for their very livelihood. And she was living like a queen.

"An ungrateful queen," he roared one day in the middle of an argument and tried to open her eyes to her failings. She was neither a good mother nor a good wife. Irresponsible and ungrateful. All the good things he offered her! She just took them for granted. No man, no man would put up with her. She did not answer but went about sulking. He ignored her even in bed and would not take her in his arms though he detected a tear or two. It was time she got some sense in her head.

The next morning there was the usual hassle with the children and breakfast. But she continued to sulk. In the evening she put his dinner on the table and went out to read on the terrace. He took no step forward. In bed, lovemaking was restrained and mechanical on both their parts. But it did clear the atmosphere, and the next morning everything was back to normal. Then two days later when Naiim asked her why she had not brought his shirts from the laundry, she suddenly snapped.

"Do you know why you keep finding fault with me?" Her voice was cool but slightly shaky. "It is your inferiority complex speaking. You know I'm too good for you."

Naiim almost had a stroke. All his blood rushed to his heart, his throat; he felt his heart would burst. She, too good for him! A good-for-nothing brat, a parasite. . . .

"Crazy! You have gone stark crazy. You've lost your mind!"

He gradually calmed down and resumed in cold anger. "And why is it that you are too good for me, may I ask?"

She would not answer.

"Is it because I'm too old for you? Is it? Answer me!" He began shouting again but forced himself to calm down. "Why did you marry me then?"

"I didn't think you would be so neurotic," she blurted. "Neurotic," a fancy word that the whores must have taught her.

He did not sleep well that night. He thought of his childhood, his father and mother, his proud youth and manhood in Baghdad. He thought of his two sisters and his brother in London. What would they think, if they saw him sunk so low in the mud? From now on he would have nothing to do with her. He would take good care of the children and see to their needs, but would have very little to do with her.

He kept his resolve. He did not talk to her except in monosyllables, on vital matters only—about the children or the household expenses. In the evenings she would put his supper on the table and roam about the apartment. He would eat in silence, occupy himself with the children, listen to the radio and go to bed. The third evening of their quarrel, after putting the children to sleep, she suddenly began to dress furtively and nervously. He saw how she held up her head, defiantly buttoned her sweater, snatched her handbag and threw the words at him.

"I'm going to my father's," she announced.

He did not answer or move a muscle as she hurried out and closed the door behind her.

He ventured out onto the terrace. A wave of cool air brushed his face and almost washed away his troubles. The sky was clear, serene. He lingered a while, then went in and settled down in the living room.

The next evening she stayed home. After the children went to sleep, she kept herself in the kitchen and baked a cake while he sat in the living room and reread the morning paper. The next evening she again left for her father's, while he stayed home with the children. His anger rose against her father and even against Marcelle. They should scold her for her leaving her husband and children and roaming about at night. The telephone rang; he answered and whoever it was hung up. It suddenly dawned on him that it was not the first time that had happened. It was most likely Doris and her sneaky ways. Good for her. He didn't care. Maybe it wasn't Doris after all. Pain twisted his chest as he picked up the phone and called Esther on a pretext about a telephone bill. She was there all right. He took his morning paper to bed, read a little and went to sleep.

Next evening was a Friday. Esther came forward and said without looking at him, "Tonight Ezra is having a party. Do you want to go?"

He did not answer.

"Did you hear what I said?"

"No, I don't want to go."

"I might go with Doris."

"Don't you dare!"

He waited for an outburst, an argument, but she went about her business. He moved from one room to the other and kept a vigilant watch. She looked sullen and moody. Would she dare join Doris? By ten o'clock he knew she was not going. He went into the kitchen, made himself a cup of tea, drank it leisurely and went to bed. He felt her lying stiff besides him. He lay stiff too, and they spent the night in silence, if not in sleep.

A day or two passed and he realized his anger was fading. He felt it mostly at night when Esther's warm young body lay within arms' reach, and he refrained. He tried to reconstruct the quarrel to justify his voluntary self-deprivation, but pictures of the early days of his marriage intruded and subdued his anger. It all seemed so pointless and he took her in his arms. His reception was lukewarm, but he doubled his efforts and there she was with her rapture.

There followed a period of peace and quiet. Esther seemed to be trying to be a good wife and mother and Naiim decided to overlook her failings. There were still the times when her social behavior irritated him—instead of putting off the men she would sometimes respond to one stupid remark with another, chuckle and toss back her head in coquettish complacency. He would point out these regrettable failures but would refrain from rekindling a quarrel. As long as she did not overdo it.

Then one day it erupted. He never suspected she had such a big mouth. A volcano!

"I have only one clean pair of underwear left," he called to her. "Where are all my clothes?"

"It's been raining. I brought the wet clothes from the laundry and hung them out but they're still wet."

"And you leave them out there all the time?"

"What do you want me to do?"

"What if it rains all week? Do you still leave them there, till next year, maybe?"

"What do you want me to do?"

"Don't raise your voice. You hang some things inside, that's what you do. You iron a few."

"You always find fault with me. 'What do you do all day long?' You always, always. . . ." She launched into a nonstop barrage of self-justification, complaints and accusations. She was tied up with the children all day long. He had two partners, but he managed to be at the office all the time. He should see other husbands. They prepared breakfast for their wives, they did the shopping, took the clothes to the laundry, the children to the doctor; they even baby-sat.

"And what do the wives do, may I ask?" he asked sarcastically.

"They just have a good time," she sneered and defiantly tossed her head.

"You've gone crazy, I see. And of course these men are the husbands of your whore friends?" They did not own a private business, he argued, so why should they care if they took days off? They were there to exploit the government or the company they worked for. Plain parasites. Did she think they worked at all? They just pimped around all day long while he broke his back, trying to provide for her and her children.

The quarrel did not develop further. Some sulking on his part and then it diffused. But soon afterwards Naiim began to notice a change in Esther's behavior. She became grouchy and quarrelsome. She would snap at him long before he found fault with her and would raise her voice about the slightest controversy. He exercised patience and resignation. It angered him that he was being reduced to the defensive, but he was fed up with purposeless draining quarrels that did not seem to benefit Esther in any way. Her choice of style also changed. She became devoted to décolleté dresses and heavy makeup. Her concern with her appearance was most apparent during the group outings. She would start way ahead of time and conduct the stages of her "toilette" in between dinner and putting the children to bed. While setting the table, clearing away the dishes or bathing the children, she would sneak in and out of the bedroom, add one touch after another, so that when she was through with the day's work, she was through with her "toilette" as well. There remained the tight dress and the high heels which she would slip on with her usual swiftness, throwing back her long neck, wetting, then parting, her rouged lips. Once he mentioned that it took her hours to dress. It was during one of these foul parties with the nasty jokes and the nonsense talk. She gave him a murderous look and left it at that. But the minute they got home she showed the extent of her aggravation:

"How could you say that it takes me hours to dress?" She spoke quietly but her voice shook. He was surprised and so amused by her anger that he could not suppress a smile. What ailed her? She must want these fools to think that her beauty was natural, in no way highlighted by elaborate combination of creams, powders, rouges. . . .

"Did you take a watch and count the time it took me to dress, did you?" She went on, mercilessly and haughtily, her long hair flying in rebellion.

He was all the more amused and felt a strong urge to take her. Lately his desire had waned—on account of the quarrels, definitely. But tonight he was back in full swing. He followed her angry eyes and flushed cheeks to bed and was met by open resentment. But he had no patience tonight, no patience to solicit and strive for her eager participation. It was enough to be on top of her, to indulge his body and relish its fulfillment.

Though Naiim avoided quarrels, there were times when he could not take any more. He was not a man to be stepped on or be stuffed in someone's pocket. Even his Moslem connections in Baghdad knew better than to push him too far, while she, a good-for-nothing, thought she could castrate him. He did not hesitate to give her a tongue lashing whenever he deemed it necessary. He was especially angry the day he invited Aunt Zebeda, Violette and Maurice for tea. Coming home around six-thirty, he found the house upside down, the children dirty, and Esther just about to make dinner.

"Didn't you know they were coming?" He smoldered as he went about tidying the apartment. "I told you days ago."

"Don't shout at me. I don't have to slave for them."

"Slave for them! When do they ever come?"

He inspected the refrigerator and the kitchen cabinets. "Not even a miserable piece of cake, not even ice cream. Just those lousy cookies."

He ran down the stairs to the grocery which luckily was open. But they had no cake. He bought half a gallon of ice cream and some butter cookies. Let there be extra cookies.

Breathless from anger and climbing the stairs, he dashed into the apartment. "I never saw such a cheap, shameless, mean person. This is the only family I have. They're generous, helpful, and this is what they get. I see how you cater to your father and to your brother whenever he comes from the kibbutz. From now on I won't have your family feasting here, not if you can't show my people proper respect."

She did not answer but went into the bedroom.

He did not sit down for dinner but gulped his food while he went about bringing order to the apartment and putting the children to bed. By the time the guests arrived, the house was tidy, and he welcomed them and led them onto the terrace. Esther busied herself somewhere in the apartment and finally made her appearance. She was cordial, but not warm. She served coffee and tea but her cool manner set the tone for the whole evening.

Somehow the incident did not swell into a big quarrel. But a few days later, an unexpected brawl got out of hand and brought out such vicious animosity that Naiim himself was shocked by it.

It happened at one of the parties. That Saturday evening, Naiim and Esther set out for the eight-block walk to Jacob's apartment. The spring air was fresh and smelled of orange blossoms. Naiim savored the coolness on his bronze face. Beside him, Esther swayed her small hips, the top of her head barely reaching his shoulders. She wore a cherry-colored light sleeveless dress and pink faux pearls which highlighted her ivory skin.

At Jacob's, Esther and Naiim were engulfed by greetings, banalities and nonsense talk. There followed the usual nuts, cake, cookies, and off-color jokes. But this time there was a special attraction. One of the men, Fouad, had taken up palm reading and was anxious to exhibit his new skill; more correctly, it was the guests who insisted on benefiting from his valuable knowledge. All gathered around him, like flies around honey.

"Read my hand, my future. My hand, my hand."

"Ladies first," he declared and Doris was the lucky first of the firsts.

He held her palm in one hand, pushed it away for an overall picture, then brought it close for details. He took his time frowning, squinting, then he bobbed his head and began murmuring to Doris.

"Oh, some secrets," Ezra said. "Better come and listen, Yehouda. The husband is entitled to hear."

"Oh, be quiet," Doris snapped. "Let him concentrate."

But Fouad's concentration seemed unimpaired by the interruption. He was all wrapped up in deciphering the signs and passing the valuable information to Doris. Naiim watched as Esther's turn came and she presented her palm for inspection. Fouad held it in both of his hands.

"He has to warm the hand in order to read it well, the charlatan," Jacob teased.

Fouad was not to be intimidated. His hands encircled Esther's and his serious expression was fixed in space. "I have to concentrate," he murmured to himself. Finally he opened his hands and exposed Esther's palm to view.

"I will have to learn palm reading," Ezra declared.

"Me too," Jacob said and Esther laughed heartily.

Fouad held Esther's hand and murmured into her hair.

Naiim felt the room swirling in front of him. Imagine such behavior back in Baghdad! He was about to straighten Fouad out and give it to him. But something held him back. He might regret his outburst. Most likely he would cool down later, see the whole thing differently and loathe himself for having stood in the spotlight and drawn further attention to his shame. But wasn't it as shameful to turn one's head and swallow like a worm? This business of keeping cool was turning men into contemptible weaklings. It was the Ashkenazi way; the latest way, since Ashkenazim mocked Middle Eastern men for their hot tempers—their actions supposedly guided by emotion, not reason. Naiim switched from fierce anger to helpless frustration. It was the thought that he could still have his outburst, any time he wanted, just by calling Fouad or meeting him face to face, that finally prevailed and made him postpone any reaction. The decision eased the ready-to-burst congestion in his head. He was unaware of the aimless chatter around him and the terrace cool air did not cool his burning forehead and cheeks. A sudden fear seized him. Did anything show on his face? It must look angry red, a clear sign for everyone. It was all Esther's fault. She was the one who put him on the spot. He loathed her and wished he could strangle her slowly, oh, so very slowly; that yellow snake-neck of hers writhing between his fingers. His eyes sought her, but she avoided his gaze, and her shrill cackling stabbed him in the heart. He forced himself to endure it until eleven, eleven-thirty, when he announced he was going home. A terrible headache was the culprit.

"Esther can stay with us," Doris suggested. "We can take her home."

"No, I'd better go home too." Esther had the sense to do the right thing.

He was out in the open air; so cool and soothing. But all he could see was the dark night, as dark as his own soul. Sadness weighed so heavily on him that at first he had no strength to broach the subject with Esther. But it was only for a moment before anger took over.

"If you think I will put up with your whoring . . . ," he shouted.

"What!"

"Yes, your whoring. Why didn't you stop him?"

"Stop him?"

"Holding your hands, warming them, whispering into your hair."

"All the women. . . ."

"But not like you. He held your hand in both of his and for so long."

"So he held their hand in one and mine in two. A big thing! Holding hands!"

"I don't care about the hand-holding. I care about the meaning, the looseness, the cheap implication."

"Shh."

A young couple walked by, arm in arm, her head on his shoulder, his mouth on her cheek. Across the street, a group of thirteen-year-olds, dressed in blue and white separates, noisily sauntered across the pavement.

"You just sat there and giggled. Didn't you hear the remarks, the insinuations? If you had a little bit of self-respect, honor, you would have stopped him and not. . . ."

"Don't bother me, do you hear? I won't have it. I won't."

For days the house fumed with Naiim's anger and despair. Where was he heading with that heartless selfish wife and that pimp of a father-in-law? Shouldn't that father talk some sense into his daughter's head? No, each time Naiim complained, the pimp came up with an excuse or even justification for Esther.

Esther went her way avoiding Naiim, or was she just ignoring him? Most of the time, he sat on the terrace alone, reading the newspaper. He had no patience for anything else, not even for the children. From time to time he would eye Esther, scrutinize her looks, figure, manners, speech, as though she were a total stranger. And strange as it was, he had no desire for her.

On Saturday morning Esther announced she was taking the children to the beach and asked if he planned to join them. He shook his head. Half an hour later, Jacob and Mary honked the horn of their new car, while Esther and the children hurried downstairs.

He remained alone and roamed about the apartment from one corner to the other. He missed the children and their commotion. He thought of Esther swaying between the men, relishing the indecent nonsense, especially now that he was not there with her. Three times he made himself a cup of coffee and leisurely sipped it on the terrace. At eleven-thirty he decided to take a walk. The streets were deserted. At such an hour, on a hot summer day, it was the beach, the pools, or the apartment. He returned home exhausted, took a shower and had hardly settled down for a nap when Esther and the children rushed into the apartment. Esther, alone, handled the after-the-beach mess—wet towels and bathing suits, rubber slippers, all filled with sand. She hustled about, her face, chest and arms glowing with a rosy tan. She bathed the children and put them to bed. Then she took a shower and threw herself on her side of the bed.

He lay immobile, apathetic, confused. He closed his eyes and thought of her shiny suntanned limbs, a contrast to her white belly and breasts. He felt exhausted to the point where nothing mattered except his own exhaustion. Was it the heat that had lulled his senses and thoughts and made him gradually sink into a deep sleep?

He woke up at two-thirty, realizing once again the blessing of a good nap. He tiptoed to the terrace and did not mind the hot waves from the west side. His present situation and his relationship with Esther did not seem so hopeless. But a slow review of her character, her irresponsibility and disregard for him, gradually renewed his anger and despair.

Esther woke up at four and the afternoon focused around the children; they played, quarreled, sulked and cried. Rena was developing into a spoiled brat, demanding special treatment from her parents and brother. Around dinnertime Esther came up to him: "There's a party at Dina's. Are you coming?" There was nothing conciliatory in her tone.

"No," he answered in an expressionless voice.

"And I suppose I can't go alone or you'll go crazy."

He chose to ignore the provocation, and she didn't pursue it either. But the extent of her annoyance was apparent in the way she snapped at the children, causing Rena to emit one shrill scream after another. Afterward she carried on a long, hushed phone conversation which certainly had to do with the party. But Naiim chose to ignore it. He went out on the terrace, leaned on the railing and watched the street. It was becoming alive again. Children gathered to play on the sidewalk in front of the building and groups of young jubilant scouts passed by. Naiim pulled up a chair, sat down and went on watching. He knew that Esther would not dare go alone to the party.

"I want to talk to you," Esther announced.

It was Sunday evening. He had just come home from work, eaten his supper and was settling down with his cup of coffee on the terrace. She had fed the children, sent them to bed; he helped in spite of himself. Then she followed him to the terrace.

"I want to talk to you," she repeated, and Naiim felt a strange satisfaction. She had finally come around from her "don't bother me. I won't hear more about it," and he would give it to her. He had rehearsed his speech more than once and hoped the message would get through. The issue was a wife's loyalty to her husband. He was the only one she could rely on, the only one who took care of her and her children; the others would offer her a flattering, smooth tongue, that was all. What would a few smooth words cost them? Nothing. Besides. . . .

"I want to tell you that this cannot go on. I won't have you harass me."

"Now, wait, wait. . . ."

But she went on with her harangue. He was smothering her, strangling her. She couldn't breathe. She couldn't talk or laugh as she pleased. He was a drag, dreary and gloomy. If it were up to him, she would never go out, neither to a movie nor a play, or even to see some friends. She would just stay home and do the housework. She couldn't go to the neighbors without his calling her back after a few minutes. She couldn't speak to a man without his becoming irritated and implying that she was acting like a whore. If he was jealous, it was his problem, not hers. She could not suffer doubly. Not only did she have an old husband, but she had to cater to his inferiority complex.

"Which whore, now which whore taught you all this?"

"How come you know so much about whores? Did you work as a pimp in Baghdad? Anyway, I don't care what you say, not any more. You want to say it's the whores who taught me. Fine, so it's the whores who taught me. You don't scare me with your talk of whores and prostitutes, not any more. And you won't take my friends away from me."

"Your friends, of course. If you paid as much attention to your husband and your household duties as to . . ."

"You and my household duties! You're so grouchy, so demanding. You married someone as young as your daughter and you expected to find a mother."

"What kind of blasphemy is that? What wife tells her husband he's old? What kind of a monster are you? Why did you marry me in the first place?"

"I didn't think you would be so neurotic."

"Listen to me. Now listen to me. I might be old but I am worth ten of you. God knows what trash, what trash you come from, or you wouldn't talk like that."

"You come from trash. It's you who comes from trash."

"Me from trash! Twaig family."

"Tussic (ass) family."

He went for her, but she flew off the terrace, through the living room to the bedroom.

"Tussic!" He ran shouting but was unable to catch up with her before she locked herself in.

He raged about the apartment and his shouts woke the children. He calmed them down and consequently calmed himself down. But Esther did not come out. He recalled Ashkenazi allusions to Middle Eastern men being emotional and wife-beaters. The allusions used to anger him as they applied only to a very few low-class men. And there he was, himself. . . . He realized that a person could be driven to almost anything. You never knew how low you could sink, he concluded and his eyes got wet. He called to Esther to come out. He would not dirty his hands by touching her. But she would not come out. He went to the children, saw to it that they fell back to sleep; then he shuffled to the terrace. The air was getting wet but it did not ease the burning in his head. Waves of anger, regret and helpless sorrow alternately seized him. Anger finally prevailed. She had gradually cheated him of all his husband's rights, but he would not let her get away with it. He would either teach her a lesson or divorce her. He would like to see if those friends of hers would lift a finger for her. He was prepared for everything. He would get the best lawyer. She always hinted that this was Israel, not Baghdad, and according to the law a wife could not be cheated of anything. Impossible laws that let a man sweat all day, allow his wife to plague him with her whims and walk off with his assets. Well, he knew something about these laws. He would never give up the house but would never invest in it either; he would keep sending his savings secretly to his brother. It was good to have foreign currency, and he would not allow this good-for-nothing brat to harvest the fruit of his labor. He would. . . . Meantime he would have to sleep on the living room sofa.

Esther came out in the morning but he hardly looked at her as he took his breakfast, dressed and hurried to work.

He came home to find the house empty. There was a note on the coffee table saying that she and the children were at her father's place. Anger shook him from head to foot. How could she do this to him? How could she take away his own children without consulting him? How could her father allow her to do that? How he hated that pimp who had fawned on him as long as he needed his rations, his home, his food. Let him feed his grandchildren now. He wondered how long he and Marcelle would stand such a commotion in a one-bedroom apartment, and the thought eased his anger. Let them suffer for a while. He would wait and see. Meanwhile he took his bath, prepared himself a supper of cheese and eggs, ate, drank his coffee, then went inside and listened to the radio. It was strange how tired he was. No wonder, with last night's sleeplessness. He settled into bed and slept soundly till morning.

Morning brought an empty feeling. But it soon dissipated as he hurried to work, work which had the power of eliminating all outside thoughts. Coming home in the evening he met Doris at the entrance to the building. She gave him an awkward, hurried greeting which confirmed his conviction that she knew all about his problems with Esther, to the last, minute detail. The encounter disturbed him and made him restless. He had no patience for another omelet for supper, and he decided to eat out. He took his shower, lingered till eight-thirty just in case Esther might call, then left the apartment, took the bus and got off at Rama Station. He was confronted by the cross section lights, the traffic jams and the line of small restaurants stretching as far as the Ramat-Gan movie house. He chose the Shemesh Restaurant, sat in the outdoor section and watched the passersby. He ordered shish kebab and relished the spicy, well-flavored meat and the soft pita bread. Such an improvement over Esther's lousy cooking. He ordered a cup of tea, dark cardamom tea, which revived his senses. He sipped it and chatted with the waiter. Then he went home. He had an urge to call Aunt Zebeda or Maurice and discuss his problem with them. After all, they were the only family he had. But it was late, and he did not want to disturb them. Besides, there was no hurry. Tomorrow would do as well.

Coming home the next evening, Naiim waited till eight o'clock for a call from Esther, her father or even Marcelle. He felt a little disturbed when he came across the children's things. Here a toy, there a small blouse, a tiny stocking. He called Maurice and met him at Aunt Zebeda's. There he got all the encouragement he needed. Aunt Zebeda did not say "I told you so." Instead, she made him feel justified in his behavior; she let him know he was a fine man in all respects and a spoiled brat should not be allowed to make a fool of him. Maurice also gave him support and both advised him to play the waiting game. Let her stay at her father's as long as she wanted. She was bound to get in contact with him. In good spirits, Naiim went home and had a good night's sleep.

But the waiting game did not prove easy. The next day, at work, Naiim found himself thinking of Esther and her shamelessness. It was even more difficult at home and he could not concentrate on the radio programs. He kept reviewing Esther's behavior, his own, their first years of marriage, their love, and the good life they might have had together if it hadn't been for her stupidity and her giddiness. It was a relief when suddenly the telephone rang, and he heard Marcelle's voice on the line.

"Oh, how are you, Naiim?" she began. "Sorry about what is going on between you and Esther. I'm sure you want to see the children. You can do that any time. Just let me know in advance."

"So I'm allowed to see my children, am I? Of all the indecent women. . . ."

"Oh Naiim, she really is a good girl, deep down. And you also are a fine man. It is just that things, misunderstandings happen, you know. I'm sure everything will be all right. And the dear children in between. Think of them. If you just talk it out. . . ."

He was unable to get anything but noncommittal remarks and Marcelle's suggestion that he come to see the dear children. It was settled that he would visit the next day, at six-thirty.

At six-thirty, Naiim rang Marcelle's bell, and as the door opened the smell of laundry chlorine filled his nostrils.

"Come on in, please." Marcelle was all smiles. "Children," she called as she seated him on the sofa; the woolen upholstery scratched his arm.

David came to him with a plastic truck in his hands. "The tire screw is loose," he said and pushed the truck for his father's inspection. Naiim seated David on his lap and kissed him on the temple.

"Come, Rena," Marcelle called. But Rena stood aside sucking her thumb, a bashful sullen look on her face. He should have brought something for the children, but all he had thought about were his quarrels with Esther. He smiled at Rena, motioned with his hand, and she slowly and shyly came over. He kissed her and seated her on the sofa beside him. It was then that Esther's father appeared, murmured an awkward *Shalom* and moved uneasily about the living room.

"Esther, dear," Marcelle called. "I put some coffee on the stove. Could you see if it's ready?"

"It's ready," Esther called back.

"Could you please bring it over?"

There was no answer, but a few minutes later Esther appeared with a tray of Turkish coffee which she put on the table. She would not deign to pass it on. It was Marcelle who took a cup and offered it to Naiim. Then everyone, including Esther, helped themselves.

"Now why don't you straighten out this whole thing?" Marcelle's honeyed voice began. "Such a shame, such nice people, both of you. So many misunderstandings just happen. And you have such beautiful children. . . ."

"Are you telling me? You'd better tell him," Esther began. "It is he who makes my life impossible. It is he who keeps pestering me. I can't speak with anyone, I can't laugh, I can't . . ."

Naiim did not care to listen. Instead he moved closer to Marcelle, snatched her thick rugged hand, held it lovingly in both of his, pushed his mouth between her ear and hair and whispered softly. Then he pulled away his hand and mouth and looked Marcelle straight in the eye. "That is what she does with those idiotic men."

"Oh well, one should . . . ," Marcelle began awkwardly.

Esther became all the more heated. "But everybody . . . what can I do . . . and would you believe he was going to hit me. He actually was going to hit me." At which comment the old bastard suddenly found his tongue and declared in a quiet but firm tone, "No husband should lift a hand to his wife, no husband."

"Did she tell you what she called me?" Naiim addressed no one but Marcelle. "Tussic family. I am from the Tussic family. Tell her about my family, Marcelle."

"Oh. . . ." Marcelle's meek features struggled for the right expression.

"What do you expect, what . . ." Esther went on and on. "Anyway, I'm not going to be treated like dirt, not any more. I speak the way

I please, I behave the way I please, and no one is going to pester me. And for the time being you'd better leave me some money for the children." The old bastard bobbed his head.

"You'd better get yourself a good lawyer," Naiim found himself saying.

"I will."

"Oh, really . . . ," Marcelle began but Naiim was already on his way out, having hurriedly kissed the children good night.

She must be crazy, Naiim thought on the way home. And the attitude of that old pimp did not help matters. He recalled her words, the way she had put the coffee tray on the table without even a *Shalom*, the way she had listed her complaints and put down her terms. Such arrogance, and to think it was Marcelle who made the first move. She will yet come to her senses. Let her hire a lawyer, let her stay with her father for a while, let her ask for money. He would send her some, but he would play it cool, and if she wouldn't let him see the children he would not beg for it. Meanwhile, he would call Maurice to ask him about a good lawyer. It was too late right now. He would see to it tomorrow; everything in good time.

"Don't you trust me?" Naiim's Ashkenazi partner asked.

"Of course I do," Naiim replied, and he actually meant it. The stout, pleasant-looking Butovski was above reproach. He was congenial, honest and fair. None of the famous Ashkenazi shrewdness. As a partner, Butovski was far from an exploiter. If anything, he allowed others to exploit him. His help was there for the asking or not for the asking, and he seldom required anything in return.

"You are so good, too good." Naiim often felt guilty.

"It doesn't matter," Butovski would reply. "Partnership is not an easy matter. You have to create an atmosphere of trust and mutual help; in the end it will be to the benefit of everyone. Because once mistrust sneaks in, it becomes a vicious circle, a malignant disease which destroys everything."

"So if you trust me as you say," Butovski said, "then confide in me. I've heard that you have marriage problems, and I might be able to help. Don't worry; even if you don't trust my discretion, I am not Iraqi. We don't move in the same circles. And believe me, it is not curiosity. I honestly want to help. Because I see it is beginning to show on you."

Naiim knew it was beginning to show on him. There was a time when work provided good distraction no matter how troubled he was, but lately he often found himself unable to concentrate, lost in thoughts, angry and anxious thoughts, about Esther and his marriage. The deterioration in his state of mind occurred after he had met with the lawyer. According to the lawyer, Esther had a claim on his property regardless of whether it was she or he who had left the marriage nest. She could claim he made her life impossible by his fits of jealousy, his mental cruelty. Judges were always sympathetic to women, especially of Sephardic origin. The unfairness of it had hit Naiim in the face and stabbed him in the heart. What kind of laws were these? A woman could torture a man, drive him out of his wits and later claim half his property. Naiim suggested devices to salvage the house from Esther's claws. He could claim he owed money on it, he could . . . all of which seemed dubious to the lawyer. Naiim began blaming himself for marrying Esther against Aunt Zebeda's good advice. He began to see himself in a very dark light: impulsive, stubborn, foolish. He had never listened to reason. He had not listened to his brother's advice to refrain from registering for the laissez-passer to Israel and wait for a passport instead. He could have come out with a lot of money, like his brother and sisters. He recalled incidents in his youth when he had been too impulsively foolish. "You're too stubborn. You never listen to anyone," the family's judgment went against him. He took it with pride as a token of manliness. Now for the first time he began to doubt its wisdom. He began to dig up events in his life when his stubbornness had played him dirty tricks, finally bringing him to this disastrous marriage with Esther. He wished to God he had married an older woman. Meanwhile, he missed Esther and the children. He would remember his first years of marriage, the time David was born and tears would come to his eyes. His sleep became disturbed. He lost his appetite and with it the will to move on.

He could not even find the strength to visit Aunt Zebeda and get the usual encouragement and confidence in his righteousness. Did it all show on him so that Butovski had begun to notice?

"It might help you just to confide in someone," Butovski urged.

"I don't know," Naiim began and suddenly he found himself pouring out all his heart, his anger, his frustrations, regrets, doubts and fears.

"Can't you socialize with different people?" Butovski asked.

"It's hard. We don't play cards. Of course there are Maurice and Violette but Esther doesn't take to them."

"One should try."

"And she claims it's not her fault that men joke around with her. But she doesn't object or put a stop to it. She actually encourages it, and I can tell you she enjoys it. Of course she denies that."

"If she denies it, take her word for it. Don't dig too deep."

"And the way she giggles at those dirty jokes!"

"Dirty jokes are everywhere. I don't know what happened. It's a new fad. But that is all you hear nowadays. And these friends of yours, maybe they want to make up for the way they were inhibited and restrained in Baghdad. Just take it easy. Don't pay too much attention to it. Sometimes if you can't stop the tide, you'd better join it. Anyway if you ever need me, I'm here, and you can count on my discretion."

It did not take Naiim long to need Butovski. Two days later, Marcelle called Aunt Zebeda with reconciliation in mind. "Isn't it time they smooth out their differences? Isn't it a shame to break up a marriage with such lovely children?"

Aunt Zebeda readily agreed. She discussed the matter with Naiim, Maurice, and Violette, and it was decided that it had better be a stranger, Butovski, who would handle the reconciliation. He would bring Naiim and Esther together. There should be no one from either family, no prejudiced person involved and no hard feelings later on.

Butovski was more than willing and he invited the couple for afternoon tea at his apartment.

Naiim arrived on time and became edgy when Esther chose to be more than half an hour late. She finally showed up with a proud, defiant air, in a yellow dress, high heels and light makeup. Butovski opened the subject with, "One should have respect and consideration for each other, and a successful marriage means hard work on both sides. I myself don't want to hear about your differences. You discuss them between you. But you have to be cool and show a great deal of patience and understanding."

"It's he who should show some understanding. It's he who should show some consideration," Esther blurted out. The arrogance! It was Marcelle who had made the first move, and she, Esther, who had come for reconciliation. "All he wants is to strangle me," she went on. "I know he is jealous. But I don't give him cause. There's nothing more I can do." And she went on with her usual litany of how she could not speak, she could not laugh, she . . . "He's jealous of my youth. He wants me to grow old before my time. It's his inferiority complex. I can't be punished for being young. It is enough that I compromise. Once a week love-making. What woman would put up with it?"

"What!" Naiim sprang up; he could not believe his ears. "Of all the . . ."

"Please, please." Butovski had a hard time getting Naiim to sit down. "I didn't hear it. It's as though I didn't hear it. It won't pass this door. Even my wife is not here. I swear to you, Naiim, it won't get past this door."

"The cause is this piggishness, this bitchery. It's only lately, with these quarrels. . . . Before, she herself used to grumble . . ."

"I understand," Butovski said. "When it comes to desire, we are all affected by so many things. That's why I keep saying love and understanding. Marriage needs a lot of work and believe me, both of you are fine people. It will be easy to overcome your differences. We all have our little craziness." And suddenly Butovski pulled Esther toward Naiim and forced them to kiss each other. He opened a bottle of wine and pushed them to drink from it. Then he proposed to drive them home.

"But I have to pick up the children," Esther said.

"I'll bring them over later on. First let me take you home." Butovski spoke breathlessly, his words pouring out of his mouth. For Naiim, it was like a bad dream. How low had he sunk? What had the world come to when a woman felt no shame discussing her man's desires and proclaiming his inadequacy in front of a stranger, his associate, his friend? It was not the new Israeli world, nor the Ashkenazi influence. It was her own selfish cruelty.

Butovski found a minute to whisper in Naiim's ear. "What has been said here will not leave this room, not through me. I know how you feel, especially since you are Sephardic."

They were finally in their apartment, and to Naiim's amazement Esther found herself at home right away. She inspected the rooms, the contents of the refrigerator. Things would never be the same. He would never regard her as an understanding, faithful helpmate. She put the kettle on the stove and brought out some cups. He would never forget her allusion to his sexual behavior. He felt his head so congested that it might burst at any moment. He decided to take an aspirin and went to the bathroom cabinet.

"Do you want some tea?" Esther called and he heard his voice answering yes. Did she want to break the ice, maybe? He himself could not approach her. He had no words for her. Another dread was gnawing at his heart. How would he, how could he, mingle again with that dreadful crowd? They knew about his problems with Esther and were probably relishing it.

Soon the children burst in with their babbling and shouting. Rena was her usual brooding self. Naiim lifted her and kissed her on the forehead. He seated David on his lap, but David was fussing about a toy airplane that he had put away somewhere before going to live with his grandfather. Esther rounded him and Rena up for their bath and Naiim helped a little. Then he went out on the terrace. The air was extremely hot though the sun had set an hour ago. Esther came out with two cups of tea. Without a word, she put one on the end table near him, took the other and sat down on the marble ledge of the terrace. He sipped from his cup and stared aimlessly into space.

"Are you taking your shower now?" he finally asked.

"No, you go first."

He went into the shower and wondered at the relief one could get from the flow of water. He came out and headed back to the terrace. The wet night air did not lessen the heat. Esther went in for her shower, dragging her big Indian-designed towel. He stayed on for a while before going to bed. The sheets were warm but his body was still cool from the shower. He lay and thought about Esther's complaint of his sexual inadequacy. How could she, when he had always attended to her needs? He knew of men whose sole concern was their own satisfaction.

Esther had finished her shower; he could hear her movements. She came into the dark room and lay down beside him. Her arm touched his and the cool flesh sent a tremor into his blood. He moved forward and they were interlaced, so strongly he thought they would never break loose. But they finally broke apart.

Naiim woke with a sore heart. His watch showed three a.m. The night was dark, heavy and dead still except for his agitated heartbeat. He tried to fall back to sleep, but Esther's complaint about his sexual inadequacy filled him again with anger and sadness. The shame and depravity! How could any decent woman advertise such a matter? While most women had a hard time achieving sexual pleasure, she always had her quick and strong orgasm, thanks to his know-how. And now she was having her sweet baby sleep while he tossed in bed, his heavy heart reluctantly beating.

The next day was a working day, and Naiim gratefully hurried to the office. Butovski was as discreet as could be. No questions and no comments, as though it was not he who had engineered the reconciliation.

Naiim came home to find a well-cooked dinner and Esther hovering about the children. He made his coffee and went to sit on the terrace. Remembering Esther's complaints, Butovski's and Marcelle's hints about his becoming more outgoing, he suggested they go to a movie or invite Maurice and Violette for a cup of tea. Esther was evasive about both suggestions, and when the children went to sleep, she suggested a walk and later a treat of "falafel"—the children could stay for half an hour without a babysitter. This was Israel, not Baghdad; if the children suddenly cried, the neighbors would calm them through the terraces or even come over to see what was the matter. It was not a bad outing, and the two of them returned home for good lovemaking and a peaceful night's sleep. The next evening, Naiim had hardly finished his dinner when Doris popped in to ask Esther about a cake recipe. Esther took her to the terrace where Doris awkwardly greeted Naiim and started a forced conversation. Then Esther suggested calling Yehouda and did so in spite of Doris's mild objections. Yehouda came over and the four of them settled for a casual quiet evening with Doris and Esther doing most of the talking. The encounter eased a sore spot for Naiim. The dreaded meetings with the group no longer seemed so threatening.

From then on it was as it had been before—the parties, the picnics, the beach outings. The group expanded, with birds of the same feather getting together and a new element, Arabic music on tape, was introduced. Naiim's attitude to the group completely changed. He decided to heed Butovski's hint: "If you can't stop the tide, join it" and began taking part in the nonsense game. He talked, teased, joked, yet sensed that his efforts were somehow snubbed, even resented, especially by the men. He was surprised but ignored that. Once he teased Ezra who was making remarks about a certain Mr. Kashkoush, supposedly a homosexual.

"Your friend, ha?" Naiim grinned. There was silence and everyone seemed to be staring at Naiim. He didn't care; in fact he was rather pleased that Ezra seemed disconcerted.

But once Esther became angry with him and claimed that his teasing was in bad taste. It was at one of the parties when Mary said that her husband Jacob liked to play with balls. Naiim looked her up and down, noted her huge breasts and buttocks, and said, "Your husband doesn't need balls."

"Oh, oh," Doris said.

"Let's go to the beach. What do you say?" Esther suddenly blurted out. Then she went on talking excitedly from one subject to another.

She seemed desperately trying to divert everyone's attention. Good for her.

"How could you say something like that?" Esther reprimanded him afterwards. "Don't you know how self-conscious she is?"

"It is all right for your friends to joke as much as they want but when it comes to me. . . ."

"But it's so different."

Was it really? They had cooked their own dirty soup, but they were not ready to swallow it, not when it came to him.

"It's disgusting," one of them had commented at the one dirty joke Naiim ever told.

"It was really disgusting," Esther later defended her friends. "It was not spicy or clever. No, just plain dirty."

Well, let them sink in their own mud. He didn't care. Yet, he gradually refrained from taking part in the nonsense game and adopted a condescending aloofness.

Meanwhile, a new problem came up. Esther began asking for what, until now, he had specifically refused. She wanted him to alternate with her in babysitting the children. He had so far agreed to hire a babysitter twice a week, and there were the visits to Doris, about once a week, when Naiim would go up every now and then to see about the children. But Esther wanted to be on the loose every night.

"Not every night," she would say. "But if it happens . . . and many couples alternate in. . . ."

Actually there were only one or two couples in the group who resorted to such a practice. The others could afford a full-time babysitter or rely on a grandma or an obliging neighbor. It annoyed Naiim to think that it was Esther's friends who urged her to nag him; he knew how susceptible she was to their influence. And he could not understand why she was not ashamed to suggest going out without him, least of all to demand it.

Once, Naiim did allow Esther to go out without him. They had been invited to a Bar Mitzvah and at the last minute the babysitter didn't show up. Naiim allowed Esther to go with Doris and Yehouda, but made it clear it was a one-time thing.

Time went by and Naiim's brokerage firm prospered. He was quite generous at home, but he made it his business to transfer money to his brother in London. Marcelle and the old pimp renewed and even increased their visits. Naiim liked Marcelle, and he knew that though she claimed impartiality, she was, deep down, on his side. Once he even thought he overheard her admonishing Esther about the group, "With them you're a completely different person. I saw that once." Meanwhile Esther became more and more coquettish.

"I had my yellow décolleté blouse on with the first button open, and his eyes just stuck there and would not budge," she laughingly told Naiim about the painter for the children's room.

Then, one evening, during a party at Jacob's, Naiim had the shock of his life. The evening started with all the word twisting, the double meanings, the wisecracks, while Esther was up to her neck in the game. Oriental music floated in the air. When a lively tune began, Jacob called for belly dancing.

"You, Esther, should know how to dance," he said.

"Why me?" she giggled nervously.

"Because you're Turkish. Most Turkish women know how to."

The conversation switched to another subject. There were the usual nuts and dried fruits on the coffee table. Then Ezra passed the plate of dates to Jacob.

"Eat," he ordered him. "Eat the dates, or you'll dwindle. You will be reduced to once a week, and your wife might divorce you."

Everyone chuckled. It was well known that dates were good for the sex drive. What kind of men were these, making jokes about such matters, and the women, laughing?

But it was only late at night after he and Esther had gone to bed that it suddenly dawned on him, and an electric twist seized his chest. They were alluding to him and his once-a-week performance. So Esther had complained to them. She had dared discuss his private, intimate behavior with a bunch of. . . . Naiim could not control the congestion in his head. He would wake up Esther and have it out with her. He would blow his top no matter what happened. He would not be reduced to a mouse, his affairs discussed in the streets. As to

Ezra and his like, he would strip them of their underwear and dress their heads with them. He tried to calm himself: maybe Esther didn't tell, after all; maybe it was just a coincidence. But the figure, once a week, was so exact. He would wake her up and ask her. It would lead to a big quarrel with the children waking up. He would do it in the morning. But why, why should he be tortured by his boiling anger while she had her beauty sleep? He tiptoed to the bathroom, closed the door and took a cold shower. It eased the burning in his veins. Then he went to bed and was lucky enough to fall asleep within half an hour. He woke up to Rena's screaming and David's calling for attention. They were grouchy and demanding in the morning. It was not the time for a quarrel, and Naiim decided to postpone broaching the subject till evening.

At work, between customers, when his Iraqi partner went out on an errand, Naiim poured out his heart to Butovski.

"Ignore it," Butovski said. "Just ignore it. It's nothing. If you ignore it, they'll lay off. But if you act sensitive . . ." And Butovski insisted that they stay after work to discuss the matter. He called his wife, told her he would be home late and made Naiim do the same. They remained in the office, and for about an hour Butovski begged Naiim to ignore the whole thing.

"You have a right to perform as much as you want or can," Butovski said. "It doesn't make you less of a man. Sex drive goes up and down, regardless of age. And it isn't shameful to discuss it. I know it's hard for you to accept that because you're an Iraqi. . . ." And Butovski confided to Naiim about his own sexual problems, those of his friends, and how none saw any harm in confiding in one another.

"If I were you, I wouldn't even mention it to her," Butovski said, "least of all make it an issue. But try to make friends with people other than this group. I think we ought to get together sometime. I'll talk to my wife about it."

Naiim followed Butovski's advice and acted as though nothing had happened. The evening went as usual: dinner, the children's commotion, coffee on the terrace. Then Esther got a phone call. She talked for a while and came over to give him the news. A member of the group, Mr. Saada, had a brother, a professional singer, who lived in Jerusalem. The brother had come over for a visit, and Mr. Saada was preparing a party for him, tonight. He was to sing there, and the group was very excited about it.

"I am going to call for a babysitter," Esther announced, rather than asked.

"But we stayed so late last night," Naiim objected mildly.

"It doesn't matter. It's such an opportunity. He's a professional singer."

"All right," Naiim said.

Esther made a few phone calls, then came back to the terrace. "Everyone I know is busy tonight. It seems we won't be able to go." She sighed and waited for an answer. But Naiim made no comment.

"I'll call Doris and tell her not to wait for us. We were all supposed to go in Jacob's car," Esther said as she walked back into the apartment to the telephone.

A few minutes later, the doorbell rang and Doris, Yehouda and Jacob dashed into the apartment. Doris came straight over to the terrace, Yehouda and Jacob following.

"Believe me, it's going to be such a party," Doris addressed herself to Naiim. "He is such a great singer . . . and believe me, I would offer to bring the children over to my place, but my neighbor keeps an eye on mine, and if they wake up, sometimes they do, and she goes over, she'll be angry to find more children, like I'm exploiting her." Doris directed her lecture to Naiim; the bitch rarely addressed herself directly to him. Naiim did not answer except to say "A wife and husband should go out together" at the beginning, but when she deluged him with her "But it doesn't happen every day . . . this is such an opportunity . . . some couples . . . ," he just looked at her and listened. His expressionless silence must have disconcerted her, for she finally began to fumble for words and turned toward Jacob and Yehouda for support.

"You, Naiim, could go," Esther said. "Last time it was I who went to the Bar Mitzvah."

"Either one of you," Doris became encouraged. "It is just a shame to miss it."

"I don't that much care about outings," Naiim chose his words carefully and could not understand how the following escaped his mouth. "Esther can go if she wants to."

"Yes, why not?" Doris jumped at the suggestion and turned to Esther. "Now go and dress quickly."

What an aggressive bitch, Naiim thought, as he eyed Doris from head to foot.

"And we won't stay late," Doris tried to console Naiim as the three of them went into the apartment, leaving him behind. The two men said they would wait in the car while Doris went with Esther to her room.

"You really can go yourself if you want to," Esther stopped and called to Naiim.

"Don't insist," Naiim was sure he heard Yehouda mumble to Esther.

Two minutes later, Esther, quick as lightning, came out of the room, dressed, wearing tons of makeup, her excitement tempered by guilt. Her eyes did not meet him as she said *Shalom* and hurried out with Doris.

Naiim's stomach contracted. What had made him utter his consent? But he was not going to torture himself about it. What could they do to her, eat her up? It was just that he hated her being seen going out alone, and he guessed that neither she nor the others would behave in a proper, decent manner. And that word of Yehouda. He should be whipped for it. Naiim felt hot waves all over his body. He thought he heard Rena sniveling and went to the children's room. It was stuffy compared to the terrace and he lifted the cover off Rena's small body. He suddenly felt very tired. He had not slept well last night. They had come home after one o'clock and his anger about Ezra's date comment had kept him awake for at least two hours. As to Yehouda's "Don't insist"? Maybe he meant it differently. Naiim relaxed as merciful sleep overcame him. He half woke when Esther came home, but went back to sleep almost immediately.

Morning came and as Naiim watched Esther hassling with the children, patiently and efficiently attending to their needs, he became worked up again. She always had the devil in her when she had a good time or was planning to have one. Why did she allow them to pressure him into letting her go? She knew very well he objected to it. Maybe it was she who asked Doris to plead her cause. And how could she swallow what Yehouda had said? Had she no self-respect? She would deny it, of course, or else say he had meant it differently. From now on there was no going out alone, no matter what. He wished he had married an older woman, a much older woman; he wished he could leave Esther and start a new life, but he remembered his anxiety at the time of their split.

"It was very nice last night, a shame you couldn't come," she threw at him as she hurried from one room to the next, playing the efficient housewife.

She wasn't going to smooth-mouth him. He would have it out with her, no matter what. She wouldn't get away with it, not with him. He had been a man in that Baghdad with the ruthless Moslems. He would not turn into a mouse now. What she actually needed was to get pregnant. She had too much time on her hands and too much time always led to mischief. He closed the door and rushed down the stairs. He would have it out with her in the evening, no matter what Butovski said.

Yehouda's sly grin greeted him at the bus station. Hardly a conversation developed except about the weather and the buses in the morning. No mention of last night's party and its wonderful singer. Then Ezra appeared, greeted Naiim and went toward Yehouda. The bus came, tardy, full and the three of them huddled at the back and held onto the rail. Ezra and Yehouda began a dialogue about the benefits of real estate, then Ezra, as though feeling bad about excluding Naiim from the conversation suddenly said, "It was very nice last night. Pity you couldn't come."

"I want you to behave with my wife exactly as I behave with your wives." Naiim felt his voice shaking. "I want you to respect her the way I respect your wives." Naiim could not help his rising voice. People turned to look.

"Please Naiim, what are you talking about?" Ezra said.

"You know exactly what I'm talking about. I'm neither blind nor deaf and you'd better. . . ." Naiim could no longer control his shouting, and the whole bus was looking at him. Yehouda started to say something, but Ezra held him back. Naiim finally calmed down but went on muttering to himself. "No decency, no respect."

Yehouda and Ezra got off while Naiim remained inside, boiling. They would tell their wives. It would reach Esther and Esther would blow up. Good for her. She should be pregnant. It might drive some sense into her head. In fact, he should go back home, right now, and see to it. He would tell Esther he had a backache and would coax her into bed before the whores would get to her and tell her about his clash with the men. And he would do her a good turn. He would tear the condom right in the middle, and with Esther's fertility she would be caught for certain. He would also tell her he might take her on a vacation to Europe. He rang the bus bell, got off and went in the opposite direction. Toward home!

III: Iraqi Jews in the United States

Uprooted

"Look at him, just look at him," the young mother fumed. "As though it's the end of the world. Look at him."

Seven-year-old "him," Eli, was lying on the floor, crying miserably, his sobs shaking his body, one leg pulled toward his face, the other stretched against the living room sofa.

Grandma did not look. She went on with her cooking, stirring the steaming rice with the starchy smell, her white hair gleaming in the late afternoon sun. She ignored the uproar, as though it did not matter or it did not concern her. To the mother the forced dead silence was as articulate and unnerving as any formal accusation: she, the mother, was at fault; the grandson, never. What a fool she had been to expect some approval, some understanding, anything but this usual partiality. So partiality it was, partiality let it be. She waited, expecting, almost hoping, for some outspoken rebuke from Grandma. Then she could blow up and pour out her anger. But no rebuke came, so she talked on.

"Look at the other kids." She shook her head. "And when I remember myself at his age. . . ."

"You were different." Grandma finally spoke. "Quite a mature girl. Everybody is not the same."

It was too mild and general a comment to justify an outburst, and the young mother, tense and nervous, remained alone with her anger.

She finally took herself out of the kitchen into the living room. A fading afternoon sun flooded the apartment and the air was hot. Israel's April was usually cooler. She watered the gardenia plant and sent Eli a furtive, scrutinizing glance. His sobs had dwindled into hiccoughs. Tears wiped by dirty hands had smeared his face, and his nasal dripping threatened to reach his mouth. The unappealing sight exasperated her; frantically she grabbed a tissue and went for his nose. He fought the intrusion and burst into a new fit of loud sobs, appalled at her insensitivity in attending to his hygienic needs, while refusing him the one thing, that very thing . . .

This time it was a small, motor-equipped airplane displayed in the window of a stationery store. He had seen it on his way back from school and, from that moment on, his whole life revolved around it and it alone. He exulted in its exquisite form, its lively colors, the motor which allowed it to circle twice and make a short flight. He described it as wondrous, magical, the ultimate toy.

"I'll buy it for you next week," the young mother had agreed, "if you're a good boy."

But he begged and bargained for an earlier date, promising exemplary behavior, plenty of chores; he nagged, sulked, then cried and demanded. She scolded, shouted and finally resorted to force; a light smack on his behind. The crying had turned into sobs, no longer because of the airplane, but because of the beating, the humiliation, the injustice. He had lain on the floor near the living room sofa.

She went about her chores, adamant about ignoring him, adamant about not feeling sorry for him; discipline above love.

The sobs had turned into passive wailing. Then suddenly they stopped. Some loud noise from the street caught Eli's attention and he hurried to the terrace to find the cause. Relieved, the mother went to help Grandma with the bean soup.

Grandma remained quiet except for some banal comments about the cooking. It had been quite some time since she had last meddled in her children's households, quite some time since she lavished her advice on them: "You are all too tense and rule-ridden. You get upset about small things. Patience. . . ." The constant accusations that she spoiled her grandchildren and that their misbehavior was the consequence finally defeated her and her suggestions dwindled, then stopped altogether.

Eli had left the terrace. A little tense, the young mother waited but would not look in his direction. Soon he came over, his brown eyes dry but red, the eyelashes wet and curled.

"I'm sorry, Mother," he murmured, awkwardly bringing his face near her cheek as though to kiss her.

"Okay." She cut him short, anticipating the purpose of his approach.

"It was just that it was so magical."

"Shall we start all over again?" she snapped.

"Why do you shout at me, why?" And the tears were near.

"Because I know what you're driving at."

"Maybe Friday, the end of this week, Mother, and I promise I won't ask for an allowance next week."

"No, thanks. You already owe me your next week's allowance."

"But how, Mother, how!"

"Don't you remember . . . I won't go into it again." She shook her head.

He shuffled away then turned to Grandma. "Grandma . . ."

"Look, dearest," Grandma apologized sadly, "I can't give you the money if Mother forbids it. You know I can't."

Grandma would not be dragged into the conflict. But the mother well knew Grandma's views on the subject: "You always give in at the end, so why not give in at the beginning and spare him and yourself." The mother sighed, acknowledging the truth of the remark, at least in most cases. It was her fault, the experts would say; she was not firm, she was not consistent; he had sensed her weakness and become manipulative. She could be firm and strict, but only for a short while,

for he would not be distracted nor would he cease aggravating, coax-
ing and begging. Punishment was hardly effective and it was a question of time before she would be exhausted and finally give in. The
experts would say that she . . .

She watched his set mouth, Grandma's detached attitude and suddenly she became alarmed. She would have to confront him alone,
and she did not have the strength for a new round. And there was
the wavering between anger and guilt; she should not have hit him.
She should have just ignored him. Then she had her inspiration. She
would give in; she would play the benevolent, magnanimous mother.
Better to save face, now that he supposedly had given up, than later
when he would be in an antagonistic mood. What would the child
experts say? It was her own vacillating behavior that caused. . . . She
was too tired to care. And he was a good boy, helpful with the house
chores, his homework done on time, while his allowance was mere
peanuts.

"Come here, Eli," she called. "I'm going to give you the money. Go
and buy the airplane but you're going to be good, you're . . ."

"Oh Mother!" He drowned her with kisses. "You want me to buy
you something from the grocery? Do you want anything before I go?"

"No, no. Go. Just go."

"Let's have some coffee," Grandma announced almost in a celebra-
tory tone. "I'll prepare it now."

Life in Eli's family, the Abadda, took its regular course, sometimes
jolly, sometimes trying, but mostly uneventful, monotonous. And
Grandma played an important role. The father owned a small pharmacy in downtown Haifa and except for Saturdays, he worked from
early morning till late at night; the young mother spent her days helping at the store, and taking care of the household. The parents had
little time for Eli, but Grandma, living just a few blocks away, was
there to fill the gap. Widowed at an early age and unselfish by nature
and culture, she lavished her love on all her family and especially on
Eli, her youngest grandchild. She was ready to satisfy all his whims
and more.

"How long will he remain a little boy?" She often had to justify herself to Eli's parents. Or was it that she felt sorry for him? "He is so intense when he wants something," she would say. "Very hard to distract him." And in an indirect, discreet way, she contributed to the peace in the household. Subtly, she came to a silent understanding with Eli; whenever he craved a toy or a game he would throw her a hint and she would supply it as a present.

But there were times when his strong will tried even Grandma's enormous patience; she would scold him, he would become arrogant, impertinent, and a non-speaking period would ensue. Immediately he would hang around her, quiet, yet alert to all her needs. He would bring her slippers when she took off her shoes or rush with the ashtray the moment she lit her cigarette. And she would melt, tears coming into her eyes. "My poor, poor darling, such an affectionate child."

"He knows how to get around you," the mother often told her.

But she would be past hearing, her love gone way up to the skies; he loved her and she adored him.

He would follow her around and watch her mend his clothes, or cook his favorite dishes. He often asked about her childhood and listened to her stories about the past, back in Iraq. He wanted to know all the details; if she had been a good girl and if her parents had loved her. He asked her about her own mother who had died a year earlier.

"Do you think she loved me?"

"Of course."

He began to cry.

"What is it, dear?" Grandma rushed to him.

"I and Cousin Dani used to steal candies from her closet."

"It doesn't matter. It was for you children that she kept her candies."

"I know. She used to give us some, but we also stole."

"It's all right. She knew how much you children love candy and she forgave you."

One day, Eli's father came home with some news. He had just met a friend whose brother, also a pharmacist, had emigrated to America.

"He's doing so well," the father said, "while all I do here is gather pebbles. Maybe we should consider emigrating."

"Nonsense." The wife dismissed the idea.

But the seed of discontent had been planted and ambition seeped in, then swelled. Information about the far-off land began pouring in, describing conditions and opportunities as rosy beyond belief. Eli's parents decided on the move.

Grandma and the relatives mocked the idea, refuted it and pointed out the defects of the land with the supposedly rosy opportunities; it was too big a country, too far, too . . . the Diaspora in the end. Then they enumerated the repercussions that inevitably would accompany such a step:

"You'll have a hard time adjusting to the new country, its different ways. Isn't it enough that we moved from Iraq to Israel?"

"You'll be alone, without family or friends, while, here, the whole family is within a five-minute walk from one another. Getting settled in a new country requires so much and you're relatively well off."

"Contentment is the true and only wealth," Grandma kept saying, her eyes often tearing. She was the most vehement in the family, sparing no occasion or effort to point out the foolishness of such a step.

The project, however, gradually took shape. From notion to possibility, to fact and to the near future. All through the arguments and discussions, Eli listened and, from time to time, declared, "I don't want to leave."

But his parents lured him with wonderful promises; his father would buy him toys; together they would explore the numerous exciting marvels of the new land; every year his mother would take him to vacation in Israel; his Grandma would visit, his aunts and cousins as well. And he was pacified into passive anticipation, if not eagerness.

Then, one evening, as the mother adjusted his pillows, she spotted his hidden face, smeared and reddened by silent tears.

"Why, dearest, what is it?" She became alarmed.

"I don't want the toys," he blurted out between sobs. "I don't want the vacations. I want to stay here. If father needs money, I will start working. I'm almost eight years old. I'll carry the vegetable boxes for the grocery man."

He was taken into the arms of both mother and grandmother, cuddled and caressed until calmed and reassured; he would see a new and exciting place, a country of wonders, and if he wasn't happy, the family would come back, his mother promised.

The next day, his aunt, briefed about the episode, laughingly teased him.

"Come here, cutie," she called. "Let's check out your back. Let's see if you really can carry boxes."

He shied away from her, but she grabbed him. "That delicate, little back." She passed her thick hands along his shirt. "Not strong enough, cutie. But your father doesn't really need money. He's just greedy, that's all. Nothing is ever enough for him." She summed up the family's view of the matter.

"Don't talk about my father," Eli snapped. "You're just jealous that you can't go to America yourself." He repeated his father's interpretation of the family's attitude.

"Oh, oh, so that's what he tells you." The aunt was on the verge of a verbal assault on the father, but Eli was already down the stairs, to his haven, the building playground where, except for school, he spent most of his time.

As the project advanced, serious matters needed immediate attention and the father and mother, themselves torn by doubts and fears, had no time to attend to Eli's apprehensions. But Grandma was there, and after the tearful episode when he suggested working for the grocery man, she completely changed her approach. In front of Eli, she no longer reprimanded husband and wife about the impending move; on the contrary, she pointed to its good aspects, to reassure Eli and alleviate his fears. And there were so many:

"I don't know the language. It will be so difficult."

"I won't have any friends."

"I'll miss you so."

She knew how to dissipate doubts, misgivings, raise hope, encourage, and thus she deprived herself of the right to complain.

There followed a period of procedures, preparations, a period of such hectic activity that the harried family was hardly aware of the full impact of the move. Finally the big day came, the day of separation and reckoning. Grandma could not afford the luxury of tears.

"I hate for Eli to see me cry," she said.

"You'll write me all the time," he insisted.

"Of course, dear."

The Abadda family emigrated into the new, big and strangely exciting country which turned out to be very demanding. The hoped-for prosperity would not come easily. Starting a pharmacy partnership required a great deal of effort, money and hardship along the way. But the family was ready for the challenge and confident about the outcome.

And Eli began his new life. He was overwhelmed by the big stores and their huge variety of toys. His parents bought him some, but he also relished browsing the stores and examining the merchandise. He was registered in a nearby public school. Since he hardly knew the language, he attended two periods of "English for foreigners," and the regular curriculum for the rest of the day.

"How was it?" his mother asked him after his first day in school.

"It seems nice," he said. "The kids are friendly. They call me 'the foreign student' and they keep asking about Israel, the schools, the soccer teams. . . ."

But Eli's attitude changed within a week; his mother noticed his grim face as he returned home from school.

"What's the matter?" she asked.

"Nothing," he almost snapped.

"Come on, tell me Eli."

"Nothing," His voice shook and tears came into his eyes.

"Please tell me."

"The kids at school are mean. They call me lazy. They say it's not true that I don't know English. I just use it as an excuse not to do any homework. They say I wear sandals instead of sneakers and that my pants are weird."

Eli's mother took him into her arms. "It takes time for the kids to get used to you. And your pants are nice. It's just that they have the Israeli style. But I'll buy you sneakers and some new pants tomorrow. And I'll go to the school and speak with the teacher."

"No, Mother, please."

"Why not?"

"They'll say I'm a sissy, Mother, no, please, promise me."

"I promise."

"Really Mother?"

"Do I ever lie to you?"

"No," he conceded.

Eli's predicament was told to his father and the few new family friends, and all voiced the same opinion: "It takes a little while, but it will be fine and very soon."

Meantime, the exchange of letters with Grandma was consistent. "Does he like it, is he happy?" Grandma inquired. The answering letters made no mention of difficulties or problems. The contact, now that lands and seas were in between, became strained and careful.

"I don't want Grandma to worry, so write to her that you're happy," the mother told Eli and he did as she asked.

The exclusion of Eli dragged on. The kids at school remained hostile toward the "foreign student" and Eli was in distress. He withdrew into his shell and going to school continued to be a strain. For distraction he had television, and of course his toys: a bunch of tiny soldiers, trucks and machine guns. The soldiers, alternating on the sofa and chairs, were marched, rounded up and shot down. Eli conducted the maneuvers on behalf of one of the soldiers, the hero "my G.I. Joe," as he called him. His mother urged him to join the neighborhood kids who played in the building's playground, but he would not listen. His exclusion became all the more pathetic toward spring as the weather grew mild, the sun glowed and the kids stayed longer in the playground. He would stand by the window and watch them play. "If I had only one friend!" he would say. His mother encouraged and urged, in vain. He had ventured with the children in school and failed; he would not try again. Desperate, his mother became forceful. One sunny afternoon, she took him by one hand, planted a ball in the other and almost dragged him to the playground. "We will just sit on one of the benches," she said. "You don't have to force yourself to join the kids. You don't have to. Just sit beside me. I said you don't have to play."

They were hardly in the playground when a classmate of Eli passed by and with complete disregard for the complexities harbored in Eli's bosom called jubilantly, "That's a nice ball, let's play."

From then on everything went smoothly, and soon it became as difficult to call Eli in for supper as it had been to push him downstairs to the playground. He began neglecting his few lines to Grandma. He had become a busy person. With the playground, television and G.I. Joe, it was hard to keep the schedule of homework, supper and shower, let alone writing letters.

The situation of the Abadda family was gradually improving but the new business made so many demands on time and money, that there was little thought of sending Eli to vacation with Grandma. Eli, himself, did not ask for it. As to Grandma's visiting, the family waited for better times; they still lived in a studio apartment and the business had yet to stand on its feet. The letters, alone, traveled back and forth, but now Eli was only a recipient. The mother found it necessary to make excuses to Grandma. "I usually write my letters when he's at school and I don't want to delay them."

Grandma made it easier. "If Eli doesn't have time to write, it means he's well settled and has friends. I wasn't so sure before. Now I am, and it makes me very happy." Then suddenly, in one of her letters, Grandma discarded her altruistic resignation and inquired. "Why doesn't Eli write? Has he forgotten me completely?"

The words touched a sense of duty in Eli. "I feel sad," he said and began to write again. But it was only for a short period. Then he sank back into his former carelessness.

Grandma did not comment again.

The Millionaire's Aide

A three-minute conversation, the exchange of a few banalities and there he was, savoring the sweet sensation of relief. He left the telephone booth and stepped into the corridor. To his right, waiters went in and out of the sumptuous Tower Hall. He took out a cigar and stuck it between his lips. His hand went into his vest pocket, extracting a small gold lighter with his initials on the side. The bluish flame threw a strange pallor over his thin fingers. He inhaled deeply, threw back his head and settled into an apathetic trance. His recent heavy oppression had turned into numb exhaustion. He was suddenly relaxed, tired and somehow estranged from his surroundings. To think that he, the president of a large investment corporation, a self-made millionaire at the age of twenty-eight, should be so affected by the petty squabbles of a demanding family? He recalled his pre-telephone-conversation state, the restlessness, the tightness of his head and neck muscles. He recalled the uneasy nights when arguments assailed his sleep—guilt and self-justification battling in his head. He recalled waking up with the edgy feeling that somewhere, something was wrong. The last three days had been the most difficult. He had expected to see the family at Shamash's funeral, but no one had shown up, perhaps because of the heavy rain. And then it dawned upon him that no one had contacted him since that Saturday. Had they accepted their setback so good-naturally, or . . . Suddenly their silence began to oppress him. It was a bad omen. He became anxious and wished he had invited his cousin's daughter in the first place; he imagined them so angry that they would have nothing to do with him anymore. He went so far as to think they might boycott his engagement party. A ridiculous thought, but it kept sneaking in and disturbing his mind. Of course, he would not capitulate. He had just held back and waited, his nerves so high-strung that even Tina, his fiancée, became concerned.

"What's wrong with you, Robert?" she had asked. "You seem so nervous lately."

It was hard work that helped him move on. The hectic preparations for the party, the multitude of small complex details, and his own eagerness for perfection kept his mind off the family. Yet he remained tense and nervous, until a little while ago when his mother called. Then everything became exciting, beautiful. But the thought that he, a mature person, a successful, self-made millionaire, could be so easily and so deeply affected, disturbed him and marred his present happiness. He dismissed it as inappropriate for the moment, to be dealt with later. Right now, there were more important matters to be taken care of.

"Robert!" His heart had leaped at his mother's call. Was it a new reprimand issued by the family with her as the mouthpiece? "Robert, son, do you need anything? I've been calling the office since noon. Neither you nor Lance was there. Do you need help? Michael said he would come and give you a hand." Was that all? He could still feel the sudden relief, like a cool breeze on sweating limbs.

"Thank you, Mother. I really don't need anything."

"Maybe you would like me to come over and see that everything is ready?"

"Oh, you, Mother?"

"Why not? It isn't every day that my son is getting engaged."

"Thank you, Mother. Thank you very much. But there's really nothing. Everything is taken care of."

"You're sure you don't want me to send Michael?"

"No, really."

Was it Brother Michael who had offered his services or was it her suggestion to smooth the family relationship? And why had he refused? He would have liked Michael to be with him right now. But no! Michael would not offer his services, or his company for that matter, without extending his sarcasm as well. And he, Robert, was in no mood for a new round. These clashes were really draining, at least for him.

He crossed the corridor to the big hall and looked at the beige-pink shag carpet and the elegant chandeliers reflected in the side mirror. The round hall was half glass-walled, overlooking the south bridge as far as New Jersey. Robert recalled the various deals which had shouldered each other for his approval, and concluded again that, if only for the view, he had made the right choice. He watched the waiters as they arranged the silver candlesticks and the potted flowers. The hall was divided in two parts: The part with the glass walls was reserved for the dinner tables; the other, two steps higher, was intended for the cocktail party. The orchestra was in one corner and, next to it, a half circle extending to the other end of the hall, was set up for cocktails and hors d'oeuvres. Waiters arranged the china plates, forks, knives and napkins. Robert watched his aide, a stout young man, supervising the orchestra, the headwaiter and the chef. A straight, persistent look and the aide promptly rushed over.

"How's everything going, Lance?"

"Very good, very good."

"Does Senator Lebel have a ride?"

"He will have."

"The other out-of-town guests, some . . ."

"I'll see to it for some of them."

"Thank you, Lance." Robert relished the mute, almost telepathic understanding. A look, a nod, a slight movement of the brows and Lance would appear for instructions. Sometimes even words were unnecessary; Lance would predict the matter in question and attend to it meticulously as if he were following specific instructions.

Contrary to the forecast for rain, it had been a bright sunny day, and now a languid, grey dusk was settling in. It was fortunate that most of the guests would be able to make it at such short notice. The club crowd would be there; so would Senator Lebel. It had been Lance's suggestion that Sunday was best if one wanted one's guests to come on short notice. For the rest, everything had worked out well: the orchestra, the food, the flowers. His fear that the party might not turn out as planned proved totally unwarranted. And yet even now, a slight overlooked detail might ruin the whole event. He should check again with Lance.

Outside the glass walls, the evening wavered between day and night. A faint dim light settled in and he could not tell whether it was the remnant of the day or the projection of electric bulbs sprinkled about the streets, buildings and park. He crossed the hall and stuck his nose against the glass wall. Below, the park was empty. The small pond was partly covered with leaves and a few sparrows hopped about. The trees barely swayed, their tops bright with lights. The sparrows jumped in and out of the pond, their wings at half-mast. It should be cool, even chilly, down there. He knew the feeling of fresh air on one's face, reviving the senses and tickling the imagination. He estimated the distance to the ground at 600 feet, the Tower Hall being five stories high. He smiled as he toyed with the idea of magically parachuting through the window and landing alone in the cool freshness of the park.

"Robert." He had not seen Lance coming by. "Your mother just called. She bought a big birthday cake for you. First she planned it as a surprise, but now she figures you might want to know when to schedule the cutting."

His twenty-eighth birthday had been last Thursday and he had had no time to celebrate it or even think about it. And there she was, his watchful, loving mother, preparing a birthday cake for him. He felt a strong urge to go to her, hug her, put his head on her shoulder and rest. Suddenly it occurred to him that she might bill him for the cake and not take it from her own large allowance. How low had he sunk, he, who tipped a chambermaid fifty dollars per week, to grudge his own mother a piece of cake for her son's birthday. He wouldn't grudge his mother the world! It was just that she had become an integral part of everything. He could deal with them one at a time, but as a group, a front, they were more than he could handle. It would be so much better if they would let go, just a little.

He caught a glimpse of himself in the mirror-paneled hall entrance: slim, medium height, black eyes, an oval face and a clear olive complexion. American girls called him cute, an interesting Latin type. Some people told him he had class and that his big black eyes were strange and hypnotic. He prided himself upon the fact that, unlike other Iraqi men, he was soft-spoken and taciturn. He liked to think that by not saying much, he gained much. And he certainly knew how to court a girl. "The other young men I went out with were boys in comparison," Tina had told him.

Tina was eight years younger than Robert. He remembered the first time he had seen her, some six months ago. He was struck by her fresh, healthy look, her clear blue eyes, honey-colored hair and milky complexion. She was of medium height, her round face and red cheeks reminding him of a fresh, delicious apple. And she promised to be as juicy, he smiled to himself.

His mother had wanted him to marry a girl of Iraqi origin. "She would be conservative, home-minded and family oriented," his mother would say and he agreed. He went out with American girls to have a good time, meanwhile searching for a suitable Iraqi bride. Nothing clicked, and he came to despair of ever finding the right person. Then he met Tina. Her uncle was a former judge, a member of the club and a widower. For the club annual ball the judge had brought Tina as his date. The moment Robert spoke with her, he concluded that she was well-brought-up, mature, intelligent, and, although American, as conservative as his own sisters.

"I think we should schedule the belly dancer right after the serving of the main dish," Lance droned into his ears.

Lance, and his "we" which Robert's mother so detested. "We!

Who does he think he is? You give him too much authority, Robert, that's the problem," she kept saying.

"We can't invite the whole world," Lance had said. "After all, it's an engagement party, not a wedding."

It was a Saturday afternoon, two weeks ago, and the family had gathered at his mother's place. With so much work at hand, he and Lance had barely made it in time for dinner. They arrived at the sound of plates and glasses as his mother and sisters set the table. As soon as everyone had sat down, the family began to dissect the party plans.

"Not to invite Cousin Bertha's daughter!" his mother exclaimed.

"I don't know how many people I have already. Please Mother, discuss it with Lance. I'm too busy to take care of everything."

"We can't invite the cousins' children," Lance intervened. "Just imagine. We have five uncles and three aunts on your side alone."

"My dear man," Michael went over to Lance and patted him on the shoulder, "I'm sorry my grandfather didn't consult with you when he conceived his tribe."

Everyone smiled except his mother. "Enough, Michael," she retorted. "I don't know who you invite on happy occasions, if not the family?"

"Do you know how many obligations a man in his position has?" Lance answered.

"Why don't you hire a bigger hall?" Sister Oz suggested, in her thin, dragging voice. "The Star, for instance."

"Do you know how many expenses a man in his position has?" Lance went on.

It was a blessing the way Lance undertook his defense, sparing him embarrassment and unpleasant explanations. No need for instructions or even hints. Lance seemed to take the words out of Robert's own mouth.

"You give him such a free hand." His mother was able to catch Robert aside. "He doesn't know who he is."

"He really should be put in his place," Sister Viola said.

But that was all. No outraged remonstrance against Lance as in the Cousin Ezra episode. What an episode! Of course Ezra had no business dropping by unexpectedly. Lance had met him at the reception desk and insisted that Robert could not be disturbed. He asked Ezra why he hadn't called for an appointment, and when Ezra wanted to wait, informed him that Robert was in an important meeting that would last for hours. Furthermore, Lance insisted on knowing the nature of Ezra's business. It turned out to be a request for a forty-thousand-dollar investment in a movie company. Lance asked for all the details, hinting that he thought it was a dubious proposition, but promising to discuss it with the firm's lawyers and notify Ezra about the result.

The incident had infuriated the whole family.

"We can't have everyone butting in whenever they feel like it," Lance argued and the "we" which had irritated Robert's family all along suddenly enraged them. There were allusions to money going to the head of certain people, allusions to empty values and family betrayal. And there were hints that Lance would not have acted that way without having been instructed to do it.

"How did he dare not notify you even though you were in a meeting?" Robert's mother said. "And since when does a cousin need an appointment? I see we have become more American than the Americans."

"I don't see why you couldn't have confronted the man with a straight 'no' instead of humiliating him in this manner?" Brother Michael observed.

But the direct attack was on Lance, "the aide," as Michael labeled him.

"How did he dare not to consult you, especially when it concerned the family?"

"The least he could have done was to offer Ezra a miserable cup of coffee."

In vain Robert argued that Ezra's project was vague and risky. That was not the issue, the family insisted; Cousin Ezra had been treated like a stranger, a man from the street, a dog. Lance had no right to throw out a cousin, a member of the family, and the aide became the target of a vehement attack which forced Robert to counterbalance with words of encouragement.

"You have such a flair for management," he told Lance.

For Robert had mixed feelings about the incident. He was genuinely sorry that Cousin Ezra had been humiliated; he would have preferred to welcome him as a guest and then refuse him. But he could not help being grateful to Lance for sparing him the embarrassment of refusal. He certainly had not given instructions to Lance, as the family seemed to suspect. It was just that Lance was an expert at guessing. He could have interrupted the meeting, which certainly was not going to last for hours; he could have told Ezra to wait; but he chose to act differently, and he, Robert, would not rebuke him. Lance might leave him in direct contact with the family, a thing to be avoided at all costs.

The family blazed on and on, and he felt low and ashamed; even his sleep was disturbed. He had just started going out with Tina and he could not help comparing her to himself. She was so uncomplicated, so confident; she would never need to hide behind someone like Lance. There was one incident which caught his attention. Tina had been offered a ticket for a ballet performance of Nureyev at Lincoln Center. The performance was on the day of the math finals, so she gave away the ticket to her friend Doris. A week later, she chanced to meet her math teacher and ask him if she could take her test two days earlier. When he agreed, she went to Doris and took back the ticket.

"But Doris had probably made arrangements already," he told Tina, "and you . . ."

"Well, it is my ticket."

"She could say once you offered it, it's no longer yours."

"What are you talking about? I offered the ticket on the assumption that I couldn't go. Once that assumption was not valid, the ticket is not available either."

Why couldn't he be like Tina? Why couldn't he value a situation, decide on a course of action and abide by it, regardless of others' views and hints, supposedly jests, so that he could not retort without sounding self-conscious and ridiculous? Why did he feel guilty whenever he refused the family a favor, no matter how unreasonable? What was reasonable and what was not, and who was to draw the line? He felt terrible when right after the Cousin Ezra episode, he became sick with the flu and the family smothered him with care and attention. The fever subsided, recurred after two days and, for three weeks, the family was in and out of his apartment, offering love, concern and service.

"What's the matter with you, old man?" Michael had teased, suggesting he could take a week off and help out at Robert's office.

Robert had felt so ashamed. He began to think he had acted rudely to Cousin Ezra and decided that, from then on, he would show more understanding toward the family. Here and there he indulged them with expensive gifts, and almost told Lance not to stand in for him with them. But time had flown by and meanwhile his sister Viola began her unrelenting singsong about her son, Bruce.

"Bruce could be your aide," she would say. "He can be as devoted and efficient as Lance."

According to her, Bruce was a sage. Eighteen years old and already a sage!

"He is very mature for his age," she would say. "If you back him with forty thousand for that textile venture, he would do beautifully. The way he explained it to me, there is a great future in this business. And you would benefit too!"

It took a great deal of his suaveness and Lance's bluntness to come out with a direct refusal and withstand the allusions to family devotion and solidarity.

But he had genuinely tried to help. He had organized projects for himself and the family, honestly believing that they would soon make it on their own, especially Michael, with his sharp intelligence and personal charm. And Robert had been more than ready to give a push. But they demanded push and plunge, push and plunge eternally. His suggestion about a chain of motels fell on skeptical ears. George, Oz's husband, said he would not leave his store for something he knew nothing about. He would first see how the business developed and then decide. As to Viola, she claimed that her Bruce had no interest in the motel business. Finally it was Michael, just out of engineering school, who took up the management of the partnership in the Cantor Motel. Overnight, Robert became the target of complaints both from Michael and Robert's own partner.

"I work twice as much," the partner would say, "and do you know what Michael answers? 'You earn twice as much.' It isn't my fault he expects your investment share too."

"I'm not going to kill myself for any job," Michael announced in his jaunty manner. "It pays a little more than an ordinary position. Big deal!"

In vain Robert explained that it was just the beginning, that the main thing was to get a footing in the business and acquire some experience. Michael was not impressed, and it was a relief when he willingly quit and a new manager took over.

There came Tina, as dazzling as a glorious May morning. The rainbow stripes of her long taffeta skirt blended with her flushed complexion. Her light blue eyes shone, her soft hair fell down her back and the tight blue blouse clung to her shapely curves. A bright fresh blossom!

"Oh, how beautiful!" Tina pointed at the flower arrangements and began a story about an exasperating hairdresser and a slow make-up girl. He followed her as she examined the beige-pink tablecloths covered with lace, the red and white roses, the carnations, the orchids, the silverware glittering against the glass walls and the fading grey twilight.

Before he knew it the guests had begun to arrive and he and Tina were caught up in handshakes, toasts, hugs, kisses and small talk. The hall sparkled with shiny dresses and gleaming jewels, highlighted against the men's black ties. His family, his relatives, friends and acquaintances went back and forth for drinks and snacks while the orchestra played one lovely tune after another.

Soon it was time to go into the dinner hall. He and Tina sat at a secluded table for two in the middle of the hall. He watched his family come by: his mother in golden brocade and Viola in light green chiffon. He wished they had been more fastidious in their choice of dress, but he had long ceased to interfere. He remembered the time he had commented on Viola's manner of dress. "You know what," she had teased, "next time I go shopping I'll take you with me. But don't forget to bring your checkbook."

Michael appeared at the hall entrance. He was so handsome, so elegant in his well-fitted black tuxedo.

"I don't want to annoy you, Robert, really," Michael had said. "But it's only an engagement party. I don't have to wear a black tie."

Robert had replied that lately, wherever he went, people wore a black tie, and Michael readily conceded.

Michael came forward, tall, dark, the silver-rimmed glasses giving him a look of poise and distinction. He pulled out the chair for Mother and then sat down, a faint smile on his face. His movements had always fascinated Robert. Tonight, toned down by the formal dress, they were as elegant and graceful as those of a fine horse. Ordinarily, you could not trace them; in a shirt and slacks, Michael moved like a black panther, swift, and virile. Robert wondered at his own tendency to compare people with animals. If he were to describe his own movements, would they be those of a mouse? A fox? No, most likely a squirrel.

Michael whispered something to Wilma, Viola's daughter, and both burst into hearty laughter.

"We ordered the catering from Marvel's." Lance's voice rang between the tables. "The manager of the Tower objected, saying he had the best food and all that, but we insisted, though it cost so much more."

Tina's amused smile sought her fiancé's. But Robert remained impassive. He didn't mind the guests knowing who had catered the food, not at all. Meanwhile he could not be accused of bad taste, since it was Lance who was bragging, Lance, who zigzagged between the tables, articulate and active, his movements too heavy for a twenty-year-old, too fast for a flat-footed person.

The orchestra leader called for attention, announced the engagement and invited the betrothed and guests onto the dance floor.

Beautiful Patricia joined the dancers and as usual Robert found her bewitching. Svelte and rather tall, with large green eyes and coal-black hair, she wore a black chiffon gown with tiny stripes of green velvet, its high collar stressing her slimness. A gold and emerald chok-er matched the color of her eyes. The black gown, the tremendous green eyes and the bare slim arms gave her the look of an exotic night bird. She certainly knew how to dress. Tina should befriend her and learn from her.

Among the friends made at the club during the past two years, Patricia and her husband had been the most congenial. The exclusive Royal Club! By now Robert was acquainted with quite a few mem-bers; more than two dozen were right here, sitting around the dance floor and having a good time. Why wouldn't they? Everything was perfect.

"Why should you care about anybody?" Michael had said when he noted Robert's concern that everything should meet the standards of his important friends. "You have your own personal life, your beauti-ful Tina. The social game is outdated. Only we Middle Easterners cling to it. These are the sixties. The clubs no longer mean much; the very fact that they allow newcomers shows they're no big deal, not any more."

"What makes you think I care?" Robert found himself objecting. "Even if I do, it's only for business."

Was it really only for business? He no longer knew. Everything was so confusing. And he wouldn't worry about it. All he knew was that somehow he cared, and that was it.

As the music stopped, Robert noticed a commotion at his Aunt Rebecca's table and saw Lance rushing over. He quietly led Tina back to their table while following the uproar with alert eyes and ears.

"So deafening, near the orchestra!" His aunt's angry voice was quite loud. "Couldn't they have found a worse place for me?"

"Tell me where you want to sit and I'll find you a chair with plea-sure." Invaluable Lance knew when to be firm and when to be mel-low. Finally, Aunt Rebecca was seated at his mother's table and Mi-chael, grinning, nonchalantly changed his seat. Bruce did not budge, and neither did his sister, Wilma—plain Wilma who was good at changing colleges and jobs but not at catching a husband.

Lance came over and whispered the unasked explanation into Robert's ear. "She's sore because we didn't invite the granddaughter."

But what about the other granddaughters? They too would have had to be invited even though they were not that close.

He looked at Tina's engagement ring, a beautiful, clear, five carat diamond. Fortune had come his way. It had sought him at the age of twenty-two and by the time he was twenty-five it had laid its full grip on him. "You're so daring, a born gambler," his family would say. It all seemed so unreal, now, whenever he remembered it: The dairy where he worked as a high school student and the partnership in the locksmith business while he was still in college working for his bachelor degree, then his own store, his chain, and that terrific boom in the Ida shares and the real estate business. He could not keep his hands off anything that smelled good, all through big loans and deals with business corporations. No more of that, though; now it was he who laid his full grip on fortune. No more risks, no more big loans, just a steady and safe widening of assets.

The orchestra played soft, popular tunes and the guests, young and old, stormed the dance floor. Lights were dimmed and through the glass walls, the stars mingled with the lights of the bridge and the far offshore. It was beautiful; the efforts had been worthwhile.

"What do we need an engagement party for?" Tina had asked. "Let's go on a trip instead."

"We'll go on a trip too, when we get married," he had answered.

The music ceased. He stood up and led Tina from one table to another, to greet the guests and be showered with warm good wishes. "Everything is so beautiful, the hall, the orchestra, the food. . . ."

"Beautiful, excellent, marvelous . . . ," Michael began raving when they approached his table. "Except that I don't hear the music well. Funny, somebody complained that it's deafening."

"Really," Tina said.

"Tell me Robert," Michael went on, "how does it feel to become a millionaire in such a short time?"

Robert ignored the remark and furtively looked about to see if anyone was listening. There they were, at it again, with Michael as the mouthpiece. And he had thought they would lay off.

"It must be great, really," George said. "When people are born rich, they don't appreciate it. They take it for granted."

"But to be a 'nouveau riche' is not good either, is it Robert?" Michael teased. "You have to work out everything by yourself, socially, connection-wise. If I were a millionaire and George was one, and Aunt Rebecca another, it would have been much easier for you, no?"

Robert felt the blood rising to his temples. With an icy smile he led Tina to the next table. This was too much. First his aunt, then Michael. Who would be next? What do they really want? They better let go; he didn't owe them anything. Michael with his insolent hints that he, Robert was an old-fashioned snob, who cared for appearances only. He had money and he was going to enjoy it. He had his personal life; it had first priority, of course. But he could afford much more and nobody could live secluded, anyway. He loved to dress elegantly; would he go and visit Aunt Rebecca each time he bought a new suit? He loved and could afford the best places—the finest restaurants, the most exclusive resorts—but when he frequented those places he found himself alone; none of his family, his old friends and acquaintances could afford them. To avoid being a loner, must he finance the whole family? At the opening weekend of the Quada Hilton, he had invited Bruce to come along. The moment he returned, his mother instructed, "Next time you go abroad, take Oz's son with you, then the others, one at a time."

As though his sole vocation in life was to satisfy the needs of each member of the family. Wouldn't it have been better if they had done something for themselves instead of just standing by, watching and criticizing everything he did? According to them, he was a snob, he had no family loyalty, he. . . . It was none of their damned business. There, he was getting worked up again, just when after his mother's call, he had vowed to be cool, to take things in good spirits and remember how the family had stood by him when he was sick. Was it his fault? Was he self-conscious and overly sensitive? If only he could adopt their technique of making insinuations, supposedly in jest, but actually for the purpose of saying what they wanted and getting away with it. To quote his mother's Iraqi proverb: "It is with a sober heart that the drunkard speaks."

How did the relationship get so strained? When had it begun to deteriorate? He remembered his youth, the days of buoyant, loving intimacy with Michael, Oz, Viola and their husbands. He remembered the days when the money began to flow in torrents, the intoxicating excitement of quick wealth when suddenly everything was within reach. The family was neither grudging nor sarcastic. He was a genius then, with a sharp flair for business, not just "a born gambler." The family proudly followed and raved about his every action. He had been invited to the National Corporation Conference, he had been photographed with actress Pamela Smith, he. . . . Then he had bought the house on Grand Bay in Sieta. It was a spacious, modern brick house, fifty feet above the water. When he had seen the living room with the large terrace overlooking the bay, he had decided he would buy the house at all cost. He moved in in early June, and for the first few months he could not get over the view, bright and fresh in the morning, languid and cool in the evening. He spent a good deal of time with the decorator and bought one designer piece after another. On evenings and weekends, Oz, Viola and their families would come over, and the newly hired maid would barbecue on the terrace, or right on the shore in front of the basement den. The children loved the place and often slept over. It had been a beautiful summer.

But soon he realized he had no privacy. He couldn't invite a girlfriend for the weekend without exposing her to the whole family; he couldn't entertain friends or business associates without ending up with a party for the whole family. Once he invited the managers of Mercantile Corporation to dinner and told his mother he would like to be alone with them. "What can I do about it?" She had suddenly turned pale. "I am not telling anyone to come. But Viola comes to see me every day. It's very sweet of her. Not all daughters are so devoted. If she comes during dinnertime, I can't chase her away." As it happened, Viola and her husband did chance to come at dinnertime and he behaved extra graciously, feeling guilty about mentioning the matter to his mother. But he gradually lost interest in the house. He cut down on entertaining at home and finally rented an apartment in the city. His mother and the maid stayed on, and the budget remained as inflated as in the time he had lived there. He never complained, but his mother found it necessary to comment regularly. "Don't be annoyed with my expenses. Your father could have been living now and you would have had to take care of two instead of one. Your poor father didn't live long enough to see you standing so well on your own feet," or "Do you know that sometimes God grants us our blessings not on our behalf, but on the behalf of others, close to us?" Then there were the never-ending instances of sons who, though not so well-to-do, had catered to their family right and left. And of course, an eldest son should be like a second father.

He would not pay attention to any more insinuations. He would make his decisions and stick to them with confidence. He would be like Tina; she would be his wife—her daily example in front of his eyes.

But where was Lance? He spotted him near Viola, his hand on her shoulder. Strange! Had the family come to accept him for what Robert wanted him to represent?

"Do you want me to arrange the exchange of your ticket, Viola?" Robert's sharp ears were able to make out Lance's words.

"Can you?" Viola's eyes glowed.

"Can't I?"

Robert smiled. Lance using his boss's connections to achieve his own aims. But Robert would not begrudge him his small victories. Lance was humble and, unlike others, so grateful.

"I'm not doing so badly after all, considering I'm only a high school graduate, and all thanks to you," he would say referring to the market tips, which Robert often gave him.

Soon there was applause and attention was drawn to Miss Whilhemina, the prima donna of belly dancers. Robert didn't know why he had given in to his mother and hired a belly dancer to entertain. There was something indecent and vulgar about the dance. It was years since he had seen such a performance but he knew Middle Eastern men and their reaction to it. They would swallow, gloat and rave, sticking their bills on the belly dancer's breasts and hips. According to Lance, it was the belly dancer's action as much as the men's, and Whilhemina would never allow such behavior. She was a high-class performer, a real artist.

The exotic music began to whine, reviving old memories of Bedouin shepherds and flute melodies in vast dry valleys. Brown and shapely Whilhemina swayed languidly. Her eyes held a distant look while her neck and arms extended upward as though in worship of an unknown God. The music moaned and Whilhemina, in a trance, swung her hips and waved her arms. Robert left his chair and reached the edge of the dance floor. He watched Whilhemina as her lips parted and her eyes clouded with rapture. Body held backward, she performed a series of swirls, her arms, hips and belly involved in a mysterious ritual. As the music accelerated, her swirls grew reckless and soon convulsive seizures shook her whole body. She shivered in anguish, a bewildered look on her face. Fascinated, Robert gulped his drink and followed her with his eyes. She straightened up, then suddenly writhed in pain, her hands holding her belly. He mused about the strange lust that consumed her body. She moved forward, then fell on her knees, her head to the ground. Knees tucked under her and neck twisted, she swirled from left to right. Her arms swept the floor seeking to break free, but to no avail! They fell back to her side and her agonized look begged for. . . . Robert rushed to help her. He brushed past the Senator, almost causing him to spill his drink. He excused himself, exchanged a few words and went to her. Her face now wore a new expression, exhausted but relaxed. One knee was already up and before he could reach her, she leapt off the floor and broke into a wild happy swirl of hips, breasts and belly. The drums grew louder and she circled the round floor, a smile on her parted lips. Her eyes glowed with excitement and she seemed unaware of anyone but herself and some strange secret which she possessed.

Robert followed her. He wanted to share her new secret. To draw her attention, he approached her, opened his arms and swayed in an imitative gesture. But she slipped by, her jingling bells mocking him.

Who did she think she was? Who was she to shut everyone out of her world? She was nothing but an entertainer, an entertainer at his party. He opened his wallet, took out a fifty-dollar bill and was about to insert it between her breasts. There was some applause. Tina was behind him, and before he knew it, the dance was over and Whilhemina dodged his hand and slipped past the cheering crowd.

He felt as if he were waking from a dream. The vision of Whilhemina was with him as he reached for the nearest chair, sat down and tried to focus on his surroundings. Slowly the guests dispersed, moved back to their seats and went on raving. "She's marvelous. She's great. A real artist."

"Attention, attention," the orchestra leader called, while a huge cake was brought in by two waiters. "Tonight, we are celebrating two happy events, an engagement and a birthday." And George, Oz's husband, rushed to the platform and motioned Robert to come up.

"Dear guests," George began, "it is my pleasure to announce. . . ." Robert reached for Tina's hand and led her to the platform amid loud applause. "And now," George went on, "I would like to call Uncle David and his wife to light two candles. . . ." What was the meaning of all this? It was an engagement party, not a Bar Mitzvah. Whoever heard of the family lighting candles at an engagement party? Robert knew of no such precedent, neither Iraqi nor American. He looked George straight in the eye, his stern glare leaving no doubt as to his meaning. But George would not heed a hint.

"And Uncle David would seat Robert on his lap," he went on, "and Robert would jump up and down, up and down. . . ." What was it now, a family history? There was no way to stop George without creating an unpleasant incident. . . . "Uncle Joseph who taught him how to play. . . ." And with each candle lighting there was hugging, kisses on both cheeks and a happy pose in front of the camera.

"Now what about the aunts who loved him and spoiled him as only Iraqi aunts know how to spoil. . . ." How embarrassing! What did Patricia or Senator Lebel think? And Tina's family? "Aunt Louise who knitted woolen scarves and hats to keep him warm. . . ." He knew of only one miserable scarf. "Last but not least, Aunt Rebecca. . . ." And she